Howl of the Brute

A Brute Story

∞

A novel by
Matthew H. Jones

Also by Matthew H. Jones

Year of the Brute

Howl of the Brute
A Brute Story

For GJ and JR

'Point me out the happy man and I will point you out
either extreme egotism, evil – or else an absolute
ignorance.'
– Graham Greene, *The Heart of the Matter*

CHAPTER 1

I lifted the lid of the wheelie bin to reveal a swirling tapestry of maggots. They were feasting on meat discarded by the butcher's stall operating outside my door, a mainstay of the market that sprawled the length of the street. A garrulous melee of tarpaulins and junk, it'd seen off repeated bids for closure and continued to trade despite woefully untenable hygiene standards. Last year five hundred schoolchildren had been poisoned by contaminated cuttlefish, an incident the traders attributed to 'dirty plates'.

I often received leaflets requesting I sign petitions safeguarding the rights of market traders, apparently under threat by bureaucratic councilmen, but their flagrant invasion of my designated bin space ensured these were quickly disposed of.

The market was a deceptively hollow proposition. The shiny panhandles and colourful toy nets suggested a treasure trove, invisible to the layman, but a cursory rummage revealed only further depths of rubbish. It baffled me just how they survived. Was there really such a market for off-brand cola and defective floor mops?

An unfamiliar ladder rested against the front of my building. Was I being burglarised? I gazed up to see a pair of legs dangling over the lip of the roof.

'Hey!' I called, intimidating no one. 'What's going on?'

The legs shifted and a head appeared. It was Jasper, my lettings agent. 'Hey buddy,' he called, his legs adjusting themselves. 'Don't worry, I'll be down *asap.*'

Rightly disgusted at 'buddy', I quickly unlatched the

3

front door and dashed inside. I lived in a bedsit on the second floor of a four-storey terrace house, the ground floor of which was occupied by a horrible second-hand clothes shop. Everything it sold was grey and soiled and I assumed it was a front for a sex trafficking operation.

I thrust my door open and winced as the handle gouged the inside wall, unsure whether that constituted 'normal wear and tear'. I occupied a single room and hated every inch of it. The walls were so damp I'd had to affix industrial sponge panels to absorb the moisture, beneath which were positioned buckets to catch the residual spill.

Thankfully the sole window overlooked the market, enabling me to deposit rotten vegetables onto the traders' heads. It was, however, single glazed and cracked, ensuring a perishing draught for nine months of the year.

It was beneath the window that I'd placed the fishtank. The fish themselves were long dead, boned and fried after I'd been bankrupted by a council tax bill, but the tank, mildewed and filled with icy water, acted as a refrigerator in which my packeted luncheon meat bobbed among wayward cabbage remnants. The broken window ensured the produce stayed cold while the tank made a handy basin whenever the water supply conked out.

I opened a tin of pork in vinegar and lit the tiny gas burner. Spongy and reconstituted, the meat cascaded into the pan and lashed me with vinegar. I jiggled it around, trying to brown it while adding salt and shredded cabbage. I was then interrupted by an abrupt thumping at the door.

'So sorry to drop in on you bud,' said Jasper, his sharkskin suit blue and gleaming. 'Just wanted to keep you in the loop.'

I didn't offer him a cup of tea lest it incurred some kind of fee. 'What's going on?' I said, his presence deeply discomforting.

'Just doing the tile inventory,' he said. 'Need to make sure they're all up there so we can renew the roofing safety certificate.'

Terror struck me immediately. 'Is that expensive?'

He drew a business card from his pocket and scribbled down the figures. This was how it was always done, the clandestine nature of the act suggesting a vulgarity in openly discussing such matters.

'It's essential I'm afraid,' he said, handing me the card. Leaving me to process the numbers he strode about the room, caressing drawer handles and work surfaces. 'I always forget what a great little space this is,' he said, lying of course.

I stared at the scrawl, trying to decipher the figures. I was being charged an inspection fee of seventy-five pounds, a roofing maintenance premium of ninety-five pounds and a share of the safety certificate application – a hundred and thirty-two pounds – that I'd share with the five other tenants.

'The area's brilliant as well,' he said, admiring the market below. 'Great local amenities.'

I was trying to tally the fees in my head but my maths was slow. Was it three hundred pounds?

'Definitely up and coming,' he said. 'Did you know they're opening a Pasta Warehouse on Plugwood Street?'

I panicked, knowing I was spectacularly overdrawn and hadn't the means by which to pay him.

'Did you want to make the payment now?' he said. 'My office can process it over the phone.'

I hesitated. 'Could I add it to my rent?' I said, knowing rent day was several weeks away.

He deliberated, his gurning jaw suggesting this was somehow an imposition. 'It's not really policy,' he said. 'Is there no way you can pay it now?'

I told him my debit card had been stolen and that I couldn't pay anything now, sorry.

'What about a part payment?' he said. 'Have you got any cash?' He'd now become serious, his manicured fingers drumming at the fishtank.

'Sorry.' I said, immensely glad to have inconvenienced

him.

He dithered for a few moments and said he'd need to make a phone call, ducking out to the hallway.

My pork was black and ruined and the vinegar had fizzled away leaving a sticky crust in the pan base. I could hear Jasper's muffled voice through the door as he negotiated my payment. It sounded like he was arguing and I wondered how he'd arrived at the figures he'd quoted me.

'Sorry about that,' he said, re-entering. 'Good news though, I've pulled some strings and managed to negotiate you a later payment date on the roof fee.'

I was momentarily elated, pleased at the service he'd provided, until I remembered the three hundred pounds I'd need to conjure out of nowhere.

'I'll add it to your rent,' he said with a laugh. 'Don't say I don't do anything for you, buddy!' He slapped me on the shoulder, still laughing. 'All fun and games, eh?'

He let himself out and knocked up the adjoining tenant, presumably to extract another three hundred pounds. Such visits were commonplace, the crippling fees written into the contract I'd signed out of desperation.

I'd been laughed out of the offices of every lettings agent in town, my financial insolvency and unemployed status immediate red flags. I'd also been refused a reference by my previous employer and my ex-landlord was dead, ensuring any record of my fiscal validity was lost. It'd thus been necessary to engage Gadswood Lettings, a sinister cabal of besuited automatons who thought nothing of plunging me into debt, bankruptcy and ruination. They operated out of a tiny office above a haberdashery, housing desperate tenants with neither security nor background checks. The contractual exchange happened quickly, the tenant invariably skipping the appendices detailing the 'ad-hoc maintenance premiums' they'd be obligated to pay.

Despite its auspicious appearance, Gadswood's

remained a viciously litigious operation, threatening terrifying legal action at the slightest murmur of consumer discontent. In the event of a tenant unable to pay the required fees they simply referred the query to a short-term loans company operating out of an adjacent office.

I'd been able to afford the fees until now; my redundancy settlement keeping me afloat while I scoured the job market and subsisted on soggy luncheon meat. The unexpected roofing fee would clean me out me, however. I *needed* a job.

CHAPTER 2

I jostled through the verminous scuffle en route to the bus stop, eager to keep my ten o'clock appointment. Swerving offers of tomato multibuys and rosewood blood pools I turned onto the high street to join the shabby consort at the bus stop. A blobby gaggle of the unemployed and the late, they were a thoroughly dispiriting bunch, alternately flustered and nonchalant. Piling like sludge onto the bus I itched all over, convinced the bin maggots had wriggled beneath my shirt cuffs. I prayed for the ruination of the butcher's stall, daydreaming of the pleasure I'd glean from the dismantling of their livelihoods.

A woman stared, her skin frayed and loose, and I scowled back. Her unsightly mouthcreases suggested a nicotine addiction that'd imbued in her a colourless sorrow. *How many fags did you have for breakfast?* I thought.

It seemed everyone was staring. They'd clocked my paranoiac scratching as I tried to rid myself of the imaginary larvae and evidently disapproved. *Stop staring, scum*, I urged, silent and maniacal.

I alighted outside a building of sharded glass and exposed metalwork that'd been under construction for three years, all of which was time wasted given the hideousness of the resultant structure. I was here for a meeting with Whamley & Poorfig, the only recruitment agency who'd not laughed in my face when contacted about job opportunities. They'd taken up my case with gusto: hardy northern resolve unfazed by my unemployability and lack of transferrable skills. 'We'll get yers a fookin' job,' they'd assured me.

The office decor was spartan: functional striplighting illuminated plastic intrays and little desk calendars gifted by rival firms. Outdoor jackets hung from a coatstand suggesting a workforce unburdened by the demands of fashion. The place was silent until a kettle boiled and a face emerged from a nearby office.

'Who's that?' it said.

I explained I was here for a ten o'clock meeting with Peter Whamley, managing director of the firm.

'Course you fookin' are. D'you know what? Completely slipped me mind.'

I said *that's fine* and Peter Whamley shook my hand, gesturing I follow him to the kitchen area.

'What're you having?' he said, dropping four teabags into a mug. 'I like my brew strong. None of yer pansy shite.'

I asked for a cup of tea, hoping I sounded gruff enough.

'How many bags?' he said. 'On a bad day I have five.'

I said one would be enough, prompting a disapproving tut. Did he think me a southern fairy?

'Fookin' bastards in the other office keep nicking our teabags,' he said, rummaging through the cupboards. 'You'll have to have one of mine.'

He scooped up a teabag and plopped it into my mug before pouring on gallons of milk.

'I leave the bag in,' he said, handing it to me. 'Makes it stronger.'

I took a seat in his office and fidgeted with my shirt cuffs, again reassuring myself the maggots squirmed only in my imagination.

Peter Whamley looked in his mid-fifties, with hair slicked back to resemble the fur of a saturated river rat. His chin was connected to his neck via a fleshy dewlap and his skin was tanned crimson from a lifelong ale bender.

'They're fookin' late again,' he said, staring at the empty office floor. 'Workshy bastards.'

He sat at his desk and opened a folder. 'So,' he started.

I fidgeted like an MP.

'You're looking for a management position.'

'That's right,' I said. 'A management position.'

His eyes drifted down my CV, turning it over expectantly. 'This it?' he said, brusque and dismissive.

I tried explaining that I also had customer service experience (I'd delivered bread as a teenager) but he told me to button it.

'I'm not a bullshitter,' he said. 'With me, what you see is what you get.'

I nodded, indulging his salt-of-the-earth schtick.

'And your CV's a big pile of shite. A great big fookin' pile of shite.'

Crushed, I tried to remain calm.

'You'd be lucky getting a job shovelling shit on a Sunday.' *Was this northern patois with which I was unfamiliar?*

'But,' he said, his lips curling into a smile. 'I'm a fookin' good recruiter. And I like a fookin' challenge.'

I said nothing, hoping he was right.

'I'll get you a management position. Even if you're managing fookin' pigs in a layby. I can get anyone a job, me.'

He made some additional notes, muttering about my CV being a 'bag o' shite' while guzzling tea and greasing his hair back. I glanced at a copy of *Silencing the Maggots: Arguments for Cruelty in Management* on his desk, prompting a deferential growl.

'Changed my life that book did,' he said, opening it at a bookmarked page. 'I was selling ulcer cream on folks' doorsteps till I read that.'

He cleared his throat and read aloud: "*...like the maggot, your subordinate will wriggle and squirm without direction. Do you nurture the maggot? No. Pour on salt and watch it die.*"

He guffawed as he read the last sentence. 'Quality, that.' he said.

Having photocopied my passport he rose and shook

my hand. 'That's all I need,' he said, seeing me to the lift. 'I'll be in touch.'

'Thanks,' I said, careful not to appear cloying. 'I appreciate it.'

He laughed and slapped me on the back. 'Don't worry about it y'bastard. I wouldn't be where I am today if I couldn't make a butty out of a shitheap.'

He left me and barrelled back into the office bellowing at his staff. *'Listen up you shower of bastards!'*

Emerging on the street below I felt an itching at my collar. I flapped at my shirt and a little white maggot fell to the ground beside me.

CHAPTER 3

All I'd done this week was steal tomatoes and complete loan applications. I'd usually borrow enough to cover the late fees on the previous loan and hope there'd be enough left for some brined mackerel or peppered buckwheat.

Thus I was understandably nervous when Peter Whamley phoned, cheeks trembling as I answered the phone. Apparently he had good news and wanted me to come into the office immediately. Could I be there today? I said *yes* and quickly dunked my shirt in the fishtank, scrubbed the vinegar stain with a bog brush and pegged it outside the window to dry.

I pulled a comb through my hair and waited for the shirt to dry while wolfing a tomato. I'd stolen it from a market trader and thus it was sludgy and rotten but it briefly mitigated my gnawing abdominal cramps. I often daydreamed about the groceries I'd buy should I acquire a job: plump, creamy butterbeans, oozing pork loaf, glistening tinned fish, all washed down with ruby goblets of Malbec. More importantly I'd be able to move out of this shithole and into a bedsit unravaged by damp. I'd been here eight months and the mould spores had wasted no time invading my lungs and crippling my sinus ducts. Each morning my throat burned with a claggy layer of mucus, searingly painful until my straining epiglottis sucked it out through my lacrimal sac.

Dressed and fed, I ran the gauntlet of market traders, hoping a fire would decimate their incomes. Joining the doughy herd of nobodies at the bus stop I assumed Peter Whamley must've found me a job, for why else might he have called? My imagination soared to dizzying heights as I envisioned the leather wallets and Beaujolais befitting of a management position.

The office was chattering today, evidently Whamley's reprimand had been heeded and the minion slugs had decided to show their sorry faces.

'Hi, can I help?'

A spoddy little admin monkey had clocked me and seemed eager to help. *You're so pathetic,* I thought. 'I'm here to see Peter Whamley.'

He stiffened, notably more obliging upon learning I had an appointment with the managing director. 'I'll let him know you're here,' he said. 'Can I get you anything? Tea, coffee…'

I pondered, conscious of the dwindling luncheon meat. 'I'd like a sandwich,' I said. 'I've had such a busy morning I've not had time for breakfast.'

'Of course, of course,' he said, dithering idiot. 'I'll be right back.'

He returned with a ham sandwich on a paper plate. The meat was pink and pocked with vermillion swirls like knots in a plank of wood. The sandwich was augmented by two pickled onions, small and translucent like angels' testes. It looked disgusting but I'd been famished for weeks and thus undiscerning about my dietary input.

'Mr Whamley's just in a meeting, he should be out shortly.'

Thanks drone, I thought, my jaws tightening around the bread.

I was made to wait for half an hour with nothing to do besides stare at Whamley's glum subordinates. They were ashen-faced and cowed, shuffling to photocopy contracts or whatever the hell recruitment agents did. I sipped my tea and pondered the kind of job I'd be gifted. Ideally I'd be a chief executive or board director; someone with power to throw around indiscriminately while being chauffeured to corporate banquets where the unemployed were made to fight for the amusement of the rich.

Peter Whamley then appeared, a smile on his weathered face. Had he bought shares in a coalmine?

'Get in here, ya bastard.' he said, ushering me into his office.

We sat down and he slurped his tea, the noise like a babbling river mouth. 'Sorry to keep y'waiting,' he said. 'Had a meeting with the bastard shareholders. Always up my arse about something, that lot.'

I said *that's fine* and he took a folder from his desk.

'First things first. Do you want the good news?'

Yes please, I said, daydreaming about peppercorn sauce.

'You, my friend, have got a fookin' job interview. How's about that then?'

I beamed involuntarily. 'Oh wow!' I said, immediately losing my cool. 'What's the job?'

He opened his file and handed me a piece of paper. 'You're going to be a back office administrative assistant,' he said, seemingly awaiting thanks. 'In a fookin' supermarket.'

My joviality quickly withered. 'I thought I was getting a management role,' I said. 'Isn't that what we discussed last time?'

He screwed up his face. 'Look,' he said. 'I've been doing this a long time. I know a pile of shite when I see one.' He held up my CV. '*This* is a fookin' pile of shite.'

I daren't argue. This was the closest I'd come to a job for three months. 'When do I start?' I grumbled, rightly resentful of having to take a position so obviously beneath me.

'Well,' he said. 'The first round or interviews are happening next week. Is Tuesday good for you?'

My mouth fell open, aghast. It was bad enough I was being spurned for managerial positions without having to beg an interviewer for a poxy admin job. 'You mean it's not definite?' I said, utterly humiliated. 'I'd have to go to an *interview*?'

'Correct,' he said. 'Two actually. The first one's a group session. If you get through that you'll be asked back for the second round.'

I shuddered with anger. Two interviews – must I be so cruelly demeaned?

Sensing my fury he grew stern, fixing me with a hardy stare. 'Listen pal,' he said. 'This is the best you're going to get, d'you understand? On paper you're a *pile of shite*.'

I reminded him of my management experience, jabbing ineffectually at my CV. 'I managed a team.' I said.

'You were made redundant,' he said. 'And your employer's refusing to give you a reference. Do you know what that means?'

I ummed and aahed. Was he being rhetorical?

'It means you need to grab this with both hands. This is a fookin' *gift*.'

I harrumphed, petulant and miffed. Without a job I'd be forced to keep washing in the fishtank, slowly succumbing to destitution before eviction found me homeless and mauled by street goblins.

'What about my other employers?' I said.

He arched his eyebrows, casting a further glance down the CV. 'Two years at Pasta Warehouse,' he said. 'What did that involve?'

I cast my mind back seven years to when I was, preposterously, more miserable than I was today. I'd finished a degree and found myself back with my parents, both desperate failures whom I'd genuinely never loved. A weak and stupid man, dad had worked on the windmills before the industry crumbled in the privatisation goldrush of the eighties. Left scrambling for work as his knowledge of patient sails fell into irrelevance, a period of decline followed during which mum initiated the first of many extramarital shagathons, rogering oakish men while dad lay half-conscious in the garage with a plastic bag over his head.

Desperate to escape the house I applied for every job I could, my worthless third-class degree already a glum and distant memory. During one such employment drive I was alerted to the opening of Pasta Warehouse, an execrable restaurant chain catering to those for whom boiled spaghetti and tomato sauce was a culinary stretch. I was subsequently employed as a tea chimp at the head office, ferrying drinks to the executives for inconceivably awful pay and nothing in the way of benefits.

'That's it?' said Whamley. 'You were a tea chimp?'
I explained that I'd also been responsible for opening the post but he stopped me, shaking a hand dismissively.

'And did you progress? Were you made senior tea chimp?'
I shook my head. In fact I'd been dismissed when the company had relocated to Burnage in a bid to exploit cheap office space.

'And that was when you got your last job?' he said.

Yes, that's right I said, neglecting to mention the year I'd spent living in a neighbour's cellar and illegally claiming disability allowance.

He turned the CV over, noting the underside was blank, and stared at me, a great pity in his eyes.

'Tuesday's good for me,' I said.

CHAPTER 4

I arrived home to find the upstairs neighbour had urinated on my washing from his window, a commonplace occurrence when the communal lavatory was out of service.

Jasper was in his car outside the building, smoking an electrofag and gesticulating into a phone. He jumped out upon seeing me.

'Hey buddy, great to see you,' he said. 'Can I come up? Need to have a quick chat.'

I wanted to say *why don't you just kill yourself?* but he had the power to evict me so I had to remain genial. I did, however, hope that one day he'd realise the hurt he'd caused and put a rope around his neck.

It'd been raining so the ceiling of the bedsit was dripping water and the sponge panels were saturated.

Jasper gazed around the room. 'Such a great little unit,' he said. 'Great potential.'

I carefully took the half sandwich I'd not eaten at Whamley & Poorfig, wrapped it in foil and immersed it in the fishtank. I reasoned it'd stay fresh for three days at least.

'Great system, buddy,' he said, observing my method. 'Shabby chic, I like it.'

I was terrified of asking them for a fridge. The last time I'd done so they'd threatened me with immediate eviction and charged me a ninety-pound 'correspondence fee' for the letters I'd received. Had I challenged the decision I'd have been liable for every minute of their solicitors' time, an outlay guaranteed to run into the thousands.

'So listen buddy,' he said. 'I've got an update for you.'

Oh no, I thought. Did they want a kidney?

'I wanted to come in person to avoid you being charged the correspondence fee.'

Thanks for nothing, I thought.

'But we've got some new guidelines I need to make you aware of. Unfortunately it means a few additional charges.'

Before I could burst into tears he produced a Gadswood-branded docket and sidled up to me like a friend. 'So as you can see, regulations are getting tighter.'

I read down the list of fees I was now obligated to pay. 'What's a seasonal entertainment subsidy?' I said.

He laughed, implying I'd made a good point. 'Great question, bud,' he said. 'It's basically a fancy name for a Christmas tip. We have an office party and our tenants make contributions as a kind of a 'thank you' for our work in keeping their costs down.'

'Is it a voluntary contribution?' I said.

'Afraid not, buddy. It's kind of a gesture of good faith, you know? Good will to all men and all that jazz.'

The list was dizzying: agency access fee, quarterly maintenance retainer, utility sourcing, municipal waste premium, trunking fee…was any of this real?

'I know it looks like a lot,' he said, patting my back soothingly. 'But we'll make it as easy as possible for you.'

I saw him out and lay in bed for a week.

CHAPTER 5

Tuesday arrived and I was summoned to a dilapidated business park in Scadmouth, a satellite office operated by the supermarket for which I was interviewing. Evidently they didn't want hoards of feckless interviewees soiling their head office, dirtying the fixtures with their grubby, weathered paws.

I shuddered to think of the competition: shabby hopefuls with peeling name stickers trying desperately to appear assertive and engaged, their suit jackets too big and their shoelaces frayed. I'd tower above them all, my management prowess quickly reducing them to quivering dust.

The office itself was unequivocally bleak. It was a relic of the 1970s with yellowing walls and dull lino, unchanged since the days of Presto and Woolworth's. Journeying up in the lift it became clear this was where the company hoarded their dimmest and ugliest trolls; forgotten pondlife too loyal and inconsequential to sack. They had their own ecosystem and power structures that remained inconceivably different to the material dynamism of their head office contemporaries. Here, respect was earned through slattern-mouthed eccentricity and stoic dedication to a job well done, irrespective of remuneration or perks.

I was ferried to the fifth floor, a gloomy, disused storage space where an assembly of chairs had been set out in a circular formation, oddly reminiscent of a torture pit. There was a clutch of rival goblins dotted about the circle, all shooting furtive glances first at me, then at each other, then back at me. Clearly mentally defective and woefully unqualified for an administrative position, I wondered if perhaps the aim was to fill multiple roles in one session.

I was right. There were, in fact, several positions to fill and the company had handpicked a gaggle of pliable halfwits grateful simply for a reason to leave the house.

Competing for the administrative assistant role was me (the obvious choice), Stephen, a racist ex-serviceman, and a recent media graduate named Jocelyn. We were made to team up and sell a hypothetical new sausage, assigning ourselves roles and responsibilities that'd maximise sales and productivity. Stephen, evidently damaged beyond therapy, remained sullen and despondent throughout, torpedoing any goodwill his military stripes may have earned him. Jocelyn, meanwhile, was a lost cause, admitting early on she was here only to placate her parents after they'd threatened to reduce her diesel allowance. This left only me, shining peerlessly by default.

After the session we muddled around an old-fashioned tea urn to nibble pig biscuits and hate each other at close quarters. I asked Jocelyn what she did with her time (she compered an indie bingo night) in an effort to appear ingratiating and amenable to the hawkeyed interviewers. Stephen stared at a wall with his mouth open.

∞

'You fookin' did it,' said Peter Whamley, tea cascading down his dewlap. 'You fookin' did it, y'jammy bastard.'

I explained how my aforementioned management experience had enabled me to overcome such formalities and he seemed marginally more convinced of my worth.

'Second round's next week. Tuesday alright?'

I said *yes, fine* and finished my tea.

'Anything else I can get you?' he said. 'Another cuppa?'

'Actually, I'd like a sandwich,' I said, somewhat

empowered. 'I've had such a busy morning I've not had time for breakfast.'

He summoned the admin spod and told him to 'get a fookin' sandwich made' while I fell on the biscuit medley he'd foolishly taken his eye off.

'Little bastard, that one,' he said, lobbing a folder at the boy's retreating head. 'Only gave him the job 'cos his mam's me therapist. I'd sack him tomorrow if I could.'
I sympathised, reminiscing about trying valiantly to sack Glynn but being scuppered by workers' rights legislation.

'Aye, it's all fookin' politics,' he said. 'You can't sack anyone these days.' He returned to the matter in hand. 'I'd like you to come in on Monday, how're you fixed?'

'Why?' I said. What more could he want with me?

'I want to talk you through the interview process, give you a few pointers. This lot can be slippery bastards.'
Considering my friendless life I agreed, reasoning it could only help my cause.

'Perfect. See you early? Ten-ish?'

I agreed and he said he'd have the kettle on, as if that were any kind of incentive. *Thanks for the boiled water*, I thought.

I arrived home to find a letter wedged in the letter flap. It was from Gadswood's and included a breakdown of the fees I was now required to pay. I read down the list: agency access fee, quarterly maintenance retainer, utility sourcing, municipal waste premium, trunking fee, everything Jasper had quoted me except now they'd included a ninety-pound correspondence fee – payment for receiving the very letter I held in my hand.

CHAPTER 6

The rain had caused the damp to spread across the ceiling, the black spores multiplying with astonishing rapidity. The ceiling was now almost totally covered, much of it having sprouted soft fungal tufts. I'd regularly don rubber gloves and scrub it off but the damp was ingrained so deeply in the walls it'd reappear within days.

I'd not slept properly for eight months; such was the severity of my sinus blockage. I couldn't breathe through my nose, instead lying in bed with my mouth open, sucking in airborne spores that caused my chest to wheeze and constrict as I gasped for air.

Early in the tenancy I'd contacted Gadswood's requesting the broken window be repaired but they'd advised it'd been unbroken when I'd moved in and thus the cost would be deducted from my deposit. The exchange had also resulted in my being charged an 'advisory fee' and a 'conference premium' amounting to over a hundred pounds, both payable immediately.

I'd contacted the Citizen's Advice Bureau regarding such flagrant violations of my tenants' rights but it transpired I had no recourse whatsoever; apparently it was my own fault for signing such an indefensible contract.

Existing in such conditions made me increasingly sick, my lungs struggling to repel the mildew and the blockage in my nostrils unshifting. I awoke each morning with my throat tarred with phlegm, guttural retching failing to shift the viscous carpet of mucus.

This crested after six months when, physically unable to breathe, I was gifted a complimentary stay in hospital. Dizzy with decongestants and intravenously hydrated I was lent a brief but convincing glow, my chalky skin momentarily rejuvenated. Expecting sympathy I told the consultant of the black mould, the freezing draught and the erratic water supply but instead of counsel he prescribed me a course of Sudafed and told me to pull myself together. Returning home I was sick again within a week, my chest constricted and the slime in my throat immovably dense. I quickly acclimatised to such conditions, however, taking the fits of breathlessness in my stride; troughs offset by the stinging peaks I'd hit after a strong blast of nasal spray.

Aside from the immobilising putrescence the room suffered a dearth of floorspace. I hadn't an armchair so instead used a tubular camping chair when not lying in bed pouring sweat. Besides the obvious discomfort it also required dismantling if I required access to the solitary cupboard that lay below.

The cupboard itself was no more than a burrow in the wall with the dimensions of a cereal box, but it was here I kept my non-perishable foodstuffs: tinned fish, brined frankfurters, powdered egg, all used only in times of dire need. Typically my dinner comprised a wedge of luncheon meat with cabbage scraps and, if I'd stolen well that day, a slow-boiled livestock turnip.

∞

I wheezed and gasped while scrubbing my work shirt, the only garment I owned not blackened by mildew. It needed to be dry by tomorrow as my appointment with Whamley & Poorfig was booked in early and it was important they regarded me as a marketable citizen. Having hung it outside the window I had little else to do so retired to bed at seven o' clock.

I awoke promptly and dressed quickly, chomping a mulchy tomato before leaving the bedsit. Today I'd be coached by Peter Whamley on interview practice, something I was clueless about given my last interview was six years prior. (I'd desperately wanted them to like me and had thus complimented the desking structure and office décor. I'd also been told an interviewer assesses you within minutes of your meeting so had appeared so cloyingly effusive as to appear mentally unhinged.) Such issues I'd raise with Whamley, relieved to have a professional fighting my corner.

I arrived at the office and was again met by the loping little spod who asked if I'd like a sandwich.

'Yes please,' I said. 'I've had such a busy morning I've not had time for breakfast.'

His hunched gait and truculent manner suggested someone utterly resentful of their position, a drone slug earning barely enough to survive. I envisaged his sorry routine: waking early to prepare dry, disgusting sandwiches before suffering the indignity of a train journey without a seat, suit jacket sagging off his shoulders like a tired old box. Despite identifying completely with his misery, I remained devoid of sympathy given how my life was immeasurably worse than his. At least *his* jacket wasn't sodden with damp and liable to aggravate his ongoing lung affliction. He slouched off and I considered throwing something at his head. Was his mum *really* a therapist?

Peter Whamley greeted me with his usual Neanderthal warmth, reverently offering tea like it contained any medicinal properties whatsoever. 'I need a brew in the mornings, me.' he said, seemingly unaware of the caricature he was portraying. 'Can't get by without a fookin' good brew.'

I nodded my agreement and took a seat. *Silencing the Maggots: Arguments for Cruelty in Business* was open on his desk and he noted my interest.

'Cracking chapter, that,' he said. 'Have a listen to this.'

He cast his eyes down the page. "*What is holiday? Holiday is time for maggots to think, relax and spend* your *money. Make a point of refusing all holiday requests.*" He guffawed. 'Fookin' great, that.'

He reiterated how the tome had changed his life. Previously he'd been a pharmaceutical salesman working on commission in a climate of recession and budget cuts. 'I couldn't sell a butcher a bicycle.' he explained, assuming I'd know what he meant. After a punishing dry spell he'd been sequestered to Plugwood Forest on a teambuilding weekend, an industry reacharound wherein delegates learnt how better to swindle the sick and the elderly.

'I was in a bad place,' he said, mithering idiot. 'I was behind on me mortgage, I'd had an affair with a chippie...'

I'd become bored and stared around the room for distractions. The walls were bare and the shelves contained nothing but unlabelled box folders. My eyes rested on a framed photograph on his desk, small and simple, of a woman. Was that his wife?

'Aye, she's me rock,' he said. 'Keeps me feet on the ground.'

I didn't say *she sounds criminally boring* because he'd become dewy-eyed. A closer look revealed a blotchy rash around her mouth and nostrils. Cold sores?

'That's me one regret,' he said, caressing the picture. 'I made me own treatments and tested 'em on her. Doctors said the damage was irreparable.'

I looked closer. Her lips were ribboned and colourless and the surrounding area was withered and grey. What had he *done* to her?

'Anyway, enough smalltalk,' he said. 'Fancy a brew? I'd do me nut without a fookin' brew.'

The spod appeared with a sandwich and set it down beside the disfigured wife. Whamley thrust a mug at him and ordered more tea. 'Five bags for me, alright?' He winked at me. 'I like a strong brew, me.'

Stop talking about brews, I thought.

I pushed the sandwich into my mouth, relishing the sustenance after the rotten tomato I'd eaten for breakfast.

'Now, let's talk about this interview you've got tomorrow.'

I mumbled sticky words but he waved dismissively. 'You have your breakfast, I'll do the talking.'

I sucked a pickled onion, the vinegar tart and pungent.

'They're a slippery bunch of bastards, this lot,' he said. 'Make sure you're on your guard.'

As he elaborated on the various types of bastards he'd encountered I felt a jab of uncertainty. I looked again at the photograph and the five teabags. Was he completely insane?

He waffled through an abusive tirade against HR and resourcing departments, claiming they were corrupt and fundamentally criminal. 'You'll be dancing with the fookin' devil,' he said, simulating horns with his fingers. 'You're going into *war*.'

I half-listened to his madness, covertly slipping the remaining half sandwich into my coat pocket while his back was turned. *That's lunch sorted for the week*, I cackled.

He adjourned the meeting after overrunning by an hour, his frenzied diatribe utterly incomprehensible by the end.

'All that make sense?' he said, seeing me to the lift.

'Yes, absolutely.' I said, discomforted by the encounter.

'Cracking. Now do me proud y'mad bastard.'

CHAPTER 7

The second interview was scheduled to take place at the company's head office, the shuffling also-rans having been weeded out during the group stages. I sat on a bench in the atrium, a steeping echo chamber of glass and marble, trying valiantly to belong. I was eyed with practiced suspicion by passing employees, groomed and sprightly as they swaggered out for fag breaks.

One day, I thought, *one day I'll be earning enough to afford a pouch of tobacco.* Such dreams were quickly supressed however, flights of fancy not conducive to a stern interview persona.

'Hey there,' came a voice. I looked up to see a limber catalogue model some ten years my junior.

'I'm Will,' he said, his handshake firm and brisk. 'Great to meet you. Shall we head upstairs?'

Okay Will I said, following him to the lifts. Tellingly, the lifts in this office were polished and digital whereas the ones in the Scadmouth office had been creaky and beige. A closer inspection of the workforce (slick, young, quick-footed) magnified the contrast.

'Very different to the Scadmouth office.' I noted, helpfully stating the bloody obvious.

'Certainly is,' said Will. 'Thank Christ.'

I laughed, glad we were on the same page. 'Do you go down there much?'

'I try to avoid it,' he said. 'They're a weird bunch.'

His derision was understandable. The Scadmouth office was, by comparison, a hole in the ground, a dilapidated eyesore groaning with box files and counting machines. The kitchens were grimy and the canteen was staffed by terrifying ex-offenders. By contrast, this office had not only a salad bar but also a designated omelette station.

'Ham, green peppers, anything you want,' said Will. 'I once had a fried egg in mine. Isn't that hilarious?'

I agreed, it was hilarious.

Presently we arrived at a row of meeting rooms, the windows frosted to retain precious privacy.

'Take a seat, I'll go and grab Paul,' he said, striding away. I stared at the walls in silence, glad they weren't festering with mould.

Paul Meakins managed the branch at which I'd be based should I secure the job. We'd not met but his telephone manner suggested a half-witted pushover I'd crush with little difficulty.

Will reappeared at the door, lithe and efficient, closely followed by Paul. It seems I'd envisaged him with some accuracy. A clingfilmed sandwich of a man, he stood at six feet, mid-forties, with a slight stoop. A cardigan hung from his shoulders and his shirt bowed at the gut, a doughy paunch spilling through the button slits. His hair was prematurely grey, inexplicably trimmed into a buzzcut while his eyes darted protuberantly behind his glasses. He greeted me with a pleading smile, tombstone-like teeth visible beneath a calamitous overbite.

'Hello there, I'm Paul, good to meet you, hehe.' he said, his handshake clammy and limp. Despite our unfamiliarity I had no doubt he was the most pathetic creature I'd ever met, his uselessness eliciting both wonton pity and bristling fury.

Hello Paul I said, repulsed by his spongy grey neck skin. Would he *really* be my manager?

They sat across from me and Paul dithered with folders and papers, clearly with no idea what to do with me.

'So,' began Will. 'Paul's the manager at our Prawnmoor

branch. He'll be interviewing you for the admin assistant role.'

Paul smiled and his tongue flashed out of his mouth, lizard-like. *You're disgusting*, I thought.

Will continued, 'I'm here as an HR representative; just note-taking, y'know, the boring stuff.'
Paul snorted a weird half-laugh, presumably in an effort to appear jocular. Could I take orders from such a wretch?

'Great, great, hehe, thanks,' he said, taking the reins. 'First thing's first, why do you want to work for us?'

Peter Whamley had prepared me for such questioning. The secret, he'd said, was to lie through your teeth and, if questioned, simply lie some more. 'They never check,' he'd said. 'Bunch of bastards.'

'I think it's a great company,' I said, lying as instructed. 'I admire the company values and would *love* to be a part of the team.'

Paul nodded, smiling gratefully at Will. 'They've been very good to me.' he said, personally invested in an organisation that'd sack him without hesitation should his pathetic obedience ever falter.

We trawled through my CV and I exaggerated, lied, embellished and bullshat, portraying myself as a vigilant super-drone with a wealth of relevant experience. Everything was framed either as a 'learning opportunity' or 'an exercise in management training', my erroneous jargon working wonders on the bumbling halfwit. I repeatedly used words like 'ostensibly' and 'remuneration', lending my lies a credence and officialdom that prompted quietly approving nods.

Concluding the interview, Paul asked if I had any questions. Whamley's demented drawl spun through my brain (*'ask them when they'll get back to you...imply you've got other interviews to get to...'*) and I took heed.

'When might I be hearing from you?' I said, back-footing the poor fool. 'It'd be handy to know...' I trailed off, hoping Whamley was right.

'Oh.' said Paul. He fussed with his papers, unprepared for such a proactive shot. Will quickly intervened, advising it'd be 'within the week'. I pretended to note this down, doodling some rubbish that looked important.

'Great, thanks,' I said, busy and aloof. 'Looking forward to it.'

We left Paul in the meeting room, idly combing through job specs and trying to appear important.

'I hope that was okay for you,' said Will. 'The shopfloor staff tend to get a bit nervous coming to head office.'

I admired his making excuses but Paul was a cretin and we both knew it.

'We'll be in touch, okay?' he said, his handshake firm and strong.

I sauntered to the bus stop with an uncharacteristic swagger. It seemed, perhaps unbelievably, that I'd succeeded.

CHAPTER 8

I'd spent the morning scrubbing mould off my trousers when Paul phoned.

'I've got some good news, hehe,' he said, laughing like he had breathing difficulties. 'We'd like to offer you the job.'

Having had several days to think it over I'd decided the job would constitute a headlong plunge into abject misery, a hellish tenure of unspeakable despair. The saving grace was my ensconcement in a back office; shelter from the filthy general public and their feckless grocery nagging. I assumed the shopfloor personnel would be on hand to resolve any such issues, wisely treating the customers like the human rubbish they were.

I accepted his offer with barely a thank you, furious at being duped into years of dispiriting grunt work. *What have I got myself into?* I thought, aggrieved at my hastiness in sourcing such hateful employment.

He blabbered on while I skulled a handful of painkillers and gnawed at a leek, desperate for sustenance after a breakfast of tepid algae water. The damp caused me to sneeze twelve times and I stuffed lavatory paper up my nose to prevent further spore infiltration. At the very least the job would enable me to afford basics like bread and salmon (scant reward for such backbreaking anguish) that would swell my cheeks after months of penniless starvation.

'Great,' he said. 'Can you come in on Monday? We'll

get your induction and your uniform sorted.'

A *uniform?* Had he mistaken me for one of the scurrying shopfloor rats?

'That's okay,' I said. 'I can wear a shirt and tie.'

'Everybody's got to wear a uniform, hehe.' he said, half-laughing as if that made it okay.

I remained unresponsive, silently hating his guts.

'If you could come in a little bit earlier, that'd be great. Is six-thirty okay?'

No, I thought, *that's too early.* 'That's fine.' I said, teeth firmly gritted.

Peter Whamley had advised I remain deferential for the duration of my probationary period (*'after that you can spit in their fookin' faces.'*) so I agreed to both the inhumane start time and humiliating uniform.

He began explaining the particulars of the role but I'd inadvertently wandered into a mould wind and was gripped by an oncoming sneeze. I grasped little of what he said, merely umming my assent after each sentence, lips pursed and trembling.

'Are you okay?' he said, pretending to care whether I lived or died.

'Mm-hmm.' I said, desperate now.

'Okay then, I'll see you on Monday, bright and early, hehe.'

I hung up the phone and thrashed out a sneeze, mucus pouring from my nostrils in vast, heaving streams. I clasped a sleeve to my nose and felt it dampen, the runoff now claggy and pale.

∞

I'd resolved to begin flat hunting in six months. I couldn't do it immediately as the deposit and fees were unaffordable without exemplary references and several thousands of pounds squirrelled away. This reminded me of the letter I'd tossed aside this morning. It lay, daunting and unopened, by the fishtank.

Unsurprisingly it was from Gadswood's; a summation of the fees I owed and the various penalties I'd incurred having defaulted on all of them. In addition to the usual correspondence fee (now ninety-six pounds in line with unfathomable new regulations), they'd added a maintenance operator's fee and an auxiliary boiler premium – an additional seventy-eight pounds – to the total.

I stared at the figures, then around the room. It was the size of a three-man tent, with floorspace lost in accommodating the hob and kitchen cupboard. The bulk of my possessions had been destroyed by my previous housemates during a period of systematic abuse whereby I'd seen photographs, heirlooms and my mother's dresses burnt, vandalised and urinated on. Besides trousers and a tin opener they'd left me with nothing. Even my telly had had the wires torn out of it.

Thankfully the students had been killed but my spell of peace had been short-lived. After trying to wrangle some semblance of an equitable life, my landlord had also died, leaving me the onerous task of sourcing an affordable flat in a rental market staffed by bloodless sociopaths.

I looked at the figures again. *Bathroom Augmentation Fee - £44.* The bathroom in question was a cupboard-sized hole in the wall with a toilet wedged in beside the shower cubicle – close enough to urinate in while washing. The showerhead itself was caked in limescale and gushed out freezing rusty water as it rattled in its fixture, often leaving me dirtier than when I'd stepped in.

Jasper had explained that prior to the 'augmentation' the bathroom was larger and had contained an actual bath (*'too old-fashioned for busy people like you'*) but the landlord had converted it into a fifth bedsit, cleverly securing himself an additional revenue steam in the process. A hurried necessity, the current bathroom was erected from chipboard and duct tape and had rotted within months.

Shortly after moving in I'd requested it be repaired but was immediately threatened with eviction and labelled a 'problem tenant', incurring a maintenance disruption fee in addition to the referencing, check-in and good faith payments for which I was liable.

Being a communal area I was required to wait, often for hours, if I required a wash. It was common for a queue to form outside the bathroom and my neighbours often jostled to secure a slot.

Like me, they were all Gadswood tenants, hungrily hoovered up after their references had fallen through or they'd been unable to provide six months' worth of payslips. Despite our domestic parallels I maintained a superiority over them, sneering imperceptibly as they traipsed the staircases with carrier bags full of dog meat.

My closest neighbour, Sheena, was a Welsh philosophy graduate who'd relocated from Newport in pursuit of a worthless master's degree. She'd assumed, somewhat naively, that her accommodation would be subsidised and her living expenses covered by working two jobs. Laughably mistaken, she'd since enrolled in black market drug trials and lost a lung after a gruesome surgical fumble. Now an incapacitated benefit claimant, she'd been blacklisted by every landlord in town, their 'no DSS' policy ensuring her applications were unanimously dismissed. The only DSS-friendly agent in the area, Gadswood had welcomed her to their roster, charging a monthly 'benefit facilitation' fee so exorbitant she was forced to abandon her studies and take a job as a community muckraker.

She was weathered and thin, undernourished and sickly, and I wondered if she'd not be better off dead. She'd once told me she'd left the gas on all night in the hope of killing herself but failed after the meter had run out. I asked why she didn't simply hang herself. 'I'm not *that* suicidal,' she said, weighing up her options. 'But I'd welcome an accident.'

It was she who commanded the shower in the

mornings and whom I'd need to outwit if I were to secure a morning wash.

CHAPTER 9

Monday arrived and I'd peeled myself from the bed an hour before I was due to leave, determined to get showered before Sheena. I squeaked down the passage and winced to hear the slow gush of the shower.

'Sheena,' I called, banging on the door. 'I need to use the shower.'

I heard a quiet murmur from inside. 'I'll not be long.' she said.

'How long?' I said, a slug curling over my toe.

She didn't answer, instead whistling a Christmas song.

I had no choice but to revert to the fishtank. I scurried back to my room, pulled off my dressing gown and submerged my head in the freezing cabbage water, soft algae clinging to my face and neck. I splashed my armpits and towelled the skin cells from between my toes, sponging the fungal residue from my navel and scrotum.

My work shirt hung from the window, conveniently blown dry by the bluster from the window crack, while my trousers lay on the bed awaiting ironing. I didn't have an iron so I'd placed a house brick in the oven, heating it overnight to ensure the hardiest of wrinkles were defeated. I removed it with an oven glove and drew it gingerly over the fabric, the brick causing sporadic burn marks but ultimately proving effective. It was all superfluous, however, given I'd be straitjacketed by a poxy staff uniform. I winced again at the horror of having to share a dress code with a slew of crowing gargoyles, all yammering about bread yeast and the fluctuating price of potatoes. My delirium was calmed at the thought of my cosy back office, resplendent in leather chairs and ring binders. Might we have our own coffee machine? I dared not dream so loftily; a tasteful dome kettle would be more than sufficient, thanks very much.

I strode into the dark morning, past the early market traders, the cold air ruddying their grizzled cheeks as they wheezed their breakfast cigs, gloved fingers clutching pillowy baps oozing with sausages.

The bus stop was comfortingly quiet; evidently the bulk of the commuter hoards started work later than I did, presumably in glamorous media offices with Chablis budgets and roof terraces.

I took a seat on the top deck and stared at my fellow passengers, all immutably depressing. They appeared wiry and cold, all office workers tinkering at their phones as if that might somehow help. The passenger in front had a cyst on the back of his neck that began weeping after we hit a speedbump, translucent slime snaking towards his collar. I followed its trail, deliberating whether it'd congeal before reaching the neckline. Frustratingly I was denied closure as he dabbed it with a tissue, temporarily cauterizing the wound. Would *anything* go right for me today?

I breathed deeply, trying to alleviate the chest constriction I'd incurred during my walk from the house to the bus stop. The damp air had left me gasping and my mother's inhaler was twelve years past its expiry date. She'd suffered chronic asthma and her wheezing was often mistaken for mating foxes, frequently drawing the neighbours into the garden with a rifle and a butterfly net.

My jaw felt wet and I wiped it dry: residual algae from my fishtank bath. Once paid I'd procure a sturdy scouring pad and get the tank spotless, I thought, buoyed by such fantasies of wealth.

I was deposited at the supermarket, a sprawling estate with a wide slanted roof and a car park the size of a football pitch. Inside was quiet, the low hum of strip lights and freezer units strangely comforting. I strode through the twinkling consumables to the customer service desk, slinging my head around in an effort to attract attention.

A short, wretched woman appeared. 'Can I help?' she said, slack-jawed and tetchy.

I stared at her uniform; a starched orange sack with the company logo stitched over the breast pocket. Her name badge identified her as 'Linda'.

'I'm here to see Paul,' I said. 'Today's my first day.'

She looked me up and down, her face the very picture of disgust. She picked up a telephone with an audible sigh. 'Paul, the new guy's here,' she said, pausing. 'Okay. Yeah, I'll bring him in.'

She replaced the receiver and came out from behind the desk. Swinging her key fob disinterestedly she advised I follow her. 'He's back here.' she said, sounding very much like she wanted to kill herself.

'Is Paul a good manager?' I said, hoping to secure an early ally.

'I'll let you be the judge of that.' she said, revealing nothing, although I reasoned that had the answer had been *yes* she'd have said so.

I followed her to the back of the shop, through an industrial plastic curtain, into the supply warehouse. I was momentarily dazzled at the hidden workings of such an enterprise, audibly cooing as we passed the box baler.

'It's fuckin' broken,' she said. 'We have to break the boxes down ourselves.'

'Sounds like fun,' I said.

'God, you're keen.' she said, obviously appalled. Her pinched face suggested the novelty of pallet trucks remained a cold and distant memory.

I affected an ambivalent shrug, eager to assert my insouciance but it didn't register. She already hated my guts.

'How long have you worked here?' I said.

'Nine years,' she said. 'My first job out of school.'

She said this with a quick belligerence, the inference being that she'd not completely wasted her life.

'Oh, okay.' I said, disagreeing completely.

We reached a door and Linda knocked. I heard a fussing from inside. We stood silent as Paul rustled and dithered. 'Two minutes,' he said, his voice sneering and nasal.

Linda shook her head, suggesting she too abhorred him. 'He'll be with you in a bit,' she said. 'I've got to go.'

I stood alone outside the door. The sign read *Store Manager: Paul Meakins*, beneath which the faint, inky outline of a penis and testicles was visible, indicating a commendable act of staff vandalism. Paul opened the door and greeted me, his handshake limper and clammier than before.

'Sorry to keep you waiting.' he said, his needling whine immediately infuriating.

Go to hell, I thought.

His office was pokey and his desk was cluttered with worthless piles of paper.

'Just having my breakfast, hehe,' he said, nodding to an enormous yoghurt tub. 'I like dairy.'

I sat in a chair as he spooned the cold cream into his mouth, finally licking the remnants off the foil lid. 'Best till last.' he joked, triggering my gag reflex.

He explained the organisational structure of the management team, suffixing every sentence with a bizarre snicker intended to mitigate his innate tediousness.

'I'll give you the tour, hehe,' he said, rising from his chair. 'Follow me.'

I noted with disgust the shapeless blue cardigan.

We traipsed around the warehouse, the baler having lost its twinkle as the looming tedium dawned on me. I'd have to come here *every day*, I thought, utterly distraught.

He gestured to the salt pallets and garden furniture with an almost paternal pride, referring to the company as 'us' and 'we' as if discussing his family.

'It's a great place to work,' he said. 'They really look after us, hehe.'

I wondered how accommodating the board directors might be should his profit margins slip.

We arrived at another door.

'This is the, er…' he screwed up his face in a hopeless attempt to be funny. 'The lavatory, hehe.'

At that moment the door opened and Linda appeared, spraying air freshener and buttoning her crotch fasteners. The smell of excrement filled my nostrils.

'Oh hello boys.' she said with a presumptuous degree of suggestion.

'You've met Linda, of course, hehehe,' said Paul, clearly nervous at the encounter. 'She's one of our cashier supervisors.'

Despite the spray the whiff of excrement sliced through the air. I quickly wiped my lips, having heard fecal particles remained airborne and could easily find their way into your mouth. *I don't want to eat your faeces, Linda.*

'Hehe, shall we move on?' said Paul, dithering idiot.

I followed him to the next door, the interior of which was arguably bleaker than the last.

'This is the staffroom, hehe.' he said, gesturing to the low-ceilinged box room, the budget for which had seemingly come out of the company's penny jar. There was a small plastic table on which sat a filthy Tupperware container, its insides rough with coagulated mayonnaise.

'I tell them to clear up but they don't listen to me,' he said, clearly the laughing stock of the entire staff. 'Sometimes you've got to do these things yourself, hehehe.' He took the container to a nearby sink and rinsed it out. *You're so pathetic*, I thought.

Beside the sink stood a microwave spattered with bean juice, crusty and dry. I envisaged Linda heating up brown slop and spooning it into her mouth with nauseating eroticism, her fingernails spotted with her own excreta.

'You know how to use one of these things?' he said,

eagerly dinging the microwave knob. His maxilla jutted out when he spoke, pinching his mouth skin and forcing his nose to wrinkle. I assured him I knew how to use a microwave, secretly thrilled at access to a reliable heat source. My luncheon meat would be *singing* after a few minutes in there, I thought.

He opened an overhead cupboard. 'This is where we keep the mugs,' he said, now surely boring even himself. 'You can bring your own or use one of these, it's up to you, hehe.' He paused, fixing me with an expectant stare. Several agonising seconds passed. Finally he spoke: 'just try not to get mugged.'

I waited, silent, lost. What had happened? I quickly tried to process the moment. Far from cautionary advice, it appeared he'd actually made a joke.

'Oh,' I said. 'No. Yes. Okay, I will. I won't.' I cartwheeled about my words, my sentence quickly crashing in on itself.

'I'll use one of those.' I said, somewhat shaken.

'Hehe.' he sneered.

It seemed he was worse than I ever could've imagined.

CHAPTER 10

The office in which I was to work was situated next to Paul's and resembled something between a prison cell and a fallout shelter. There were two desks; one for me, the other for staff reprimands and shoplifter interrogations.

'This is where the magic happens, hehe.' said Paul, gesturing to my desk. It was small and bare, empty besides a plastic intray and a bulky desktop computer.

He patted the computer and sniggered. 'No naughty videos, hehe.'
I assured him I'd not be watching pornography at work and he sniggered again.

'Can't be too careful, hehe.' Had my predecessor spent their days masturbating?

My uniform comprised a grotesque orange fleece and a polyester polo shirt. Heartbreakingly it was mandatory despite my days being spent in a back room, counting beans and juggling the grunts' holiday requests. Remembering *Silencing the Maggots*, I resolved to decline every single one of them, advising they learn the value of a hard day's graft instead of dallying about in swimming trunks.

Other than checking the payroll figures my duties were nominal; primarily box-ticking and float counting while occasionally cleaning the toilet or washing the dishes. Such labour was carried out by the staff both as an austerity measure and to maintain the illusion of autonomy. The theory suggested a workforce that cleaned and maintained its own store was likelier to take pride in their work and thus invest personally in the brand.

Paul then showed me around the store and introduced me to the vermin whose payslips I'd fudge. Blobby no-hopers, pustuled students, women with webbed feet, all were sickened to meet me.

'Another prick.' said a huge thug named Salman, fully aware I could hear him.

I'll botch your wages this month, I thought, surreptitiously compiling a list of expendables.

Dean mistook me for a head office store inspector, jokingly requesting a pay rise. I didn't correct him, instead adding him to my list of disposable waste.

I spent the afternoon completing induction forms and leafing through corporate training materials, quietly grumbling at the imposition. I didn't bother to even skim read them, instead skipping straight to the end and signing indiscriminately, as if it mattered one tiny jot.

Parched and sluggish, I ventured to the staffroom to make a cup of tea. I could hear laughter from inside; slow-witted natters and effusive blethering. Through the thin slit of glass I could see Linda and Salman seated at the table, both cradling mugs of commoners' tea and guzzling sugar biscuits. They fell silent as I entered, communicating with almost imperceptible nods and tics. I clicked on the kettle and stood staring at the teabags, unsure whether to engage them in smalltalk. I *was* their superior, after all. Must I fraternize with the peasants?

'You don't drink that *green* shit, do you?' asked Linda. Was she talking about algae water?

'No,' I said. Did she mean green tea?

'Last guy brought in all sorts. Chameleon tea or something.'

Salman fell about, helpless with laughter, his vast bulk caused the table to clatter. '*Camomile* tea.' he said, panting between guffaws.

Linda smiled, empowered by her assumed stupidity. 'I

dunno, do I?' she said, lapping up the adulation.

'You're something else, Linda,' he said, his eyes dewy with mirth. 'Something else.'

I tried to join in their feckless idiocy, smiling cautiously at her mistake. Sensing my eagerness Salman composed himself and eyed me coldly.

Linda spoke. 'So you drink proper tea like the rest of us?'

It seemed we were split by class divisions. Despite my lowly standing, they perceived me as an authority figure to be feared and resented by the troglodyte mass. Equally I looked upon them as contemptible filth, base and primitive.

I said *yes, I drink proper tea* and turned to face the wall. The kettle was excruciatingly slow to boil but its barrelling crescendo eventually silenced their sneers. I sped through the brewing process, the teabag barely given time to steep before I hurried back to my office. I could hear them cackling once I'd left, mocking and jeering like pigs.

I finished the day in a state of calm boredom, mentally untaxed but daunted at the prospect of having to do it all again tomorrow. I'd been spooked by Linda and Salman and spent the return journey fantasising about having them sacked. Unfortunately it seemed Linda was a shopfloor perennial, one who'd presumably banked plenty of goodwill among the workforce and thus much trickier to despatch. Salman, according to his employee record, was a relatively new starter, having been there a paltry eight months. *I mustn't act hastily*, I thought, resolving to traverse my first week before pursuing any such vendetta.

I arrived home to find the ceiling bowing over the bed. It'd rained earlier and I concluded the rainwater must've collected in the roof. Fearing a night time soaking I slept squashed up on the floor, my spine twisted and my head jammed against a table leg.

∞

Arriving at work the next day I found the store closed and a cluster of staff idling outside. Most of them were chuffing cigs and murmuring like little trolls.

'Paul's running late,' said Linda, noting my approach. 'He's the only one with keys.'

Okay, I said, grateful for any time spent not working. I leant against a trolley corral, staring at the ground in the hope none of them would talk to me. Their sallow features recalled the atrophied hunchbacks that haunted the Scadmouth office, causing me to wonder if the leap from shopfloor laggard to admin automaton really was the career progression the company trumpeted in its recruitment literature.

There seemed more of them today. Had they, like aphids, multiplied exponentially? I dreamt of an insect repellent powerful enough to silence Linda's slatternly whine. If I could weaponise it I'd seal them in the staffroom and gas them all to death.

'He's done this a lot recently,' said Linda, flanked by a chorus of murmurs. 'I wonder what he's up to?' Evidently she was the ringleader, mouthpiece for the frenzied gremlin army.

'I don't trust him.' said Salman.

Dean shook his head, his tiny brain struggling to keep up.

'Probably gonna get us all sacked,' said Linda. 'Replace us with robots.'

You'd deserve it, I thought, hoping one day they'd be enslaved by robots.

A gravelly crunch signalled an approaching car.

'That's him,' said Linda. I noticed her face twist and pinch. 'La-di-da, too good for the fuckin' bus.'

Paul fumbled out of the car and stuttered something about box junctions, quickly placating the disgruntled mob. It was then I realised how he used his odious personality to his advantage, essentially boring his assailants into submission. He also elicited an intangible revulsion, an unquantifiable disgust that caused one to recoil on contact.

'Another day, another dollar.' said Linda.

I hate it here, I thought.

Once inside I closed the office door, insulated against the disgusting general public. During my stint at Pasta Warehouse I'd been required, like all their office staff, to work in one of their branches at Christmas time, waiting on customers and shadowing the front-of-house employees. Besides ruining Christmas, the initiative succeeded only in demoralising the branch employees, who believed we'd been sent by head office to spy on them and weed out candidates for dismissal.

It was during such a secondment that I experienced the truly abhorrent face of the public at large: a flabby, facetious pretence of entitlement that believed itself righteous, proper and correct at all times. Having been playfully dubious of the 'the customer is always right' maxim, I valuably learnt that not only was the customer always *wrong*, they were, in fact, loathsome, reprehensible filth deserving of the absolute worst of everything.

I was interrupted by a knock at the door. *Go away*, I thought as Paul bustled in wearing his disastrous cardigan.

'Hiya,' he said, his overbite deeply unsettling. 'Sorry about earlier, hehe.'

Drop dead, I thought. 'That's fine.' I said.

'I was up in head office, had an early meeting with, uh, top brass, hehe.'

Was he trying to *impress* me?

'So there's probably going to be a few changes in the team, hehe. Might need you to work a few late nights over the next few weeks if that's okay?'

I remembered Whamley's advice: *stay deferential till you pass your probation* and assented. 'No problem,' I said. 'That's fine.'

He snickered and for a moment I glimpsed his devious side. Festering beneath the dorkish exterior was a man prepared to bleed and squeeze me, fully aware my probationary success lay squarely in his hands.

'Hehe, great.' he said, moving closer. His breath was hot and milky. 'Could you do me a favour?' he said, as if I had any choice in the matter. 'Could you set up some employee records for me?' He handed me a heartbreaking wad of documents and snorted weirdly.

'Okay,' I said. 'When do you need them by?'

His bulbous eyeballs rolled about behind his glasses. 'Asap sir, asap. Hehe.'

His yoghurt breath caused me to edge away. 'Yep, not a problem.' I said. He literally could've asked me anything – I just wanted him to go away.

'I'll leave you to it then, hehe.'

I watched him leave the room, wishing I had the courage to cut his brake cables. I eyed the pile of documents he'd given me. It comprised at least twenty new employees, leaving me to wonder if there'd be enough space in the fridge for all the extra Tupperware. Sifting through the folders I recognised a name. *Stephen Maltby: Customer Services Assistant.* It was the ex-serviceman I'd been teamed with during the group interview, he who'd stared at the wall with such peculiar reticence. I stared at the scuffed chairs and shabby wallpaper and wondered how the store could justify taking on twenty new employees before acknowledging that I didn't care a jot.

∞

I spent the remainder of the day pawing at papers before clocking off early and roaring to the bus stop, satisfied at what might generously be considered a day's work.

Arriving home my heart froze to see Jasper's car parked outside. Might I be liable for his parking costs?

'Hey buddy,' he said, meeting me on the stairs. His suit was ultramarine today, glossy like fish skin and augmented by a thick yellow tie. 'Don't mind me, just a bit of maintenance.'

Curiously, he was retracting a tape measure and seemed in a hurry to leave. Had he been measuring his penis?

Predictably, there was an envelope stuffed under my door with Gadswood's logo stamped on it. It itemised the agency fees for which I was currently liable: agency hospitality cross-charge, unilateral referencing stipend, ad-hoc measuring fee, all of which were, of course, payable immediately. I tossed it out of the window and collapsed on the bed. Staring at the ceiling, my eyes focused on a thin, almost invisible pencil line in the mould. It began above the door, ran the length of the ceiling and disappeared down the opposite wall. Barely noticeable, it was only the disturbed mildew tufts that drew me to its presence. I rose up and stood on the bed, craning for a closer look. Had it always been there? I moved towards the window and peered from a distance. It was like the outline of an invisible partition that effectively split the room in two. I assumed it was the remnants of a wall that'd previously divided the building and thought little more about it. I thought instead about dinner, which tonight comprised a clump of wet cabbage and a mug of rusty water.

CHAPTER 11

The pigsty grind had taken full effect after week one. I no longer sought reward in trivial victories like catching the early bus or salting Linda's tea, instead accepting my boredom with a sad and resigned solemnity. My shoulders became hunched and I affected a slight shamble when I walked, for I had nowhere to be that was worth hurrying to.

The store had quickly and effortlessly broken my spirit, its ashen ceiling tiles bearing down on me like clouds of deathly slate. Linda and Salman continued their petulant sideswipes, addressing me variously as 'Your Majesty' and 'Lord Wanker', somehow convinced I was a class tourist unburdened by financial pressures and there simply to sneer at unskilled shop workers. I explained how my parents had fallen into insolvency and that we'd been forced to clamp strangers' cars to make ends meet but they rolled their eyes, unconvinced.

'Fuckin' Rolls Royces I bet,' said Linda, ratified by Salman's thick laugh. 'Bet he went to a posh school n'all.' she said.

In a further effort to disparage myself I played down my perfectly pleasant schooldays. 'They hosed us with drain water,' I said. 'And threw us in hedges.'

They said *yeah, yeah* and continued scoffing chips.

In truth, my school years had been woefully average. I'd attended St. Muggin's Comprehensive, a former public school that'd fallen on hard times after its headteacher had absconded with thousands of pounds in school funds. The local council had begrudgingly bailed it out, albeit with far less than what was required, compelling the school to hire cheap, unsavoury and often unqualified teachers, most of whom turned out to be paedophiles.

∞

I'd created employee records for the twenty new staff and was required to contact them in the event of any missing documentation. Stephen Maltby, it transpired, had returned none of the required paperwork, presumably too immersed in war re-enactments to bother with such correspondence. I telephoned him, inexplicably nervous. Might he call me a nancy boy?

'It's me.' he answered, his voice clanging like an old bell.

Stuttering around the issue I quickly explained who I was and what I required.

'Well alright then.' he growled.

'So, do you think you could send the forms back this week?' I said.

'I'll do it,' he said. Then again, softly: *'I'll do it.'*

I thanked him and hung up. Strangely, my neck was sweating.

I contacted the remaining employees and requested their paperwork but Stephen Maltby's voice kept tolling through my head. I remembered him as tall and stocky, bald, with eyes slightly crossed and ears that protruded like marshmallows. He'd not specified which area of 'the services' he'd been involved in and I'd been loath to probe further, such was his arch and stony detachment. I'd also noticed how he kept clenching and unclenching his fists as if preparing to give me a thumping.

Paul had specifically advised I not mention the new intake to the shopfloor staff; apparently he wanted to brief them in his own time. *Fine by me*, I thought, dreading even the briefest of human contact.

The time in question arrived on a Friday, supposedly

when they were at their most malleable. Paul assembled us in the warehouse, where Linda held court among her coven of dimwits and Salman cackled vampishly. I assumed they were mocking me in some form or other. More accusations of financial stability?

Paul stood at the front, unanimously ignored. There were nebulous clusters of chat, some coughing, some mithering. A cowed and pathetic creature, he wielded no authority whatsoever, his noncommittal hushing quickly lost in the hum. Having finished her anecdote ('*I ain't walking that far for a shit.*') and lapping up the resultant hawing, Linda puckered her lips and signalled for silence. The chatter dissipated and each head turned to Paul.

'Thank you, Linda, thank you.' he said, weak and browbeaten. She wore a coy smile, her eyebrow cocked and devious.

'First of all, thanks for coming guys, hehe.'
Salman nudged Linda and she nodded, a smile brushing her lips.

'So for kick-offs I've got some good news.'
A murmur rippled through the group.

'The baler's been approved for repair. So no more cabling boxes yourselves.'

'Fucking *yes!*' cried Dean. (Was he here on community service?) The rest of them nodded and smiled. A few even patted each other's backs. Evidently this kind of non-event mattered in their miserable little world.

'Good news, good news, I know.' he said, lathering them up.

'Get in the baler!' shouted Salman, his viciousness blanketed in jest. The rest of them gurned and hooted, tickled by the camaraderie.

'Hehehehe,' gibbered Paul stupidly, grasping for a rejoinder. 'Maybe after the appraisals, hehe.'

The goodwill was immediately extinguished. *You're not one of us,* they thought.

'Anyway,' he continued, already having lost the room.

'The big news is we're getting some new starters.'

This was met with a flurry of natters. Linda had probably told them robots were being enlisted.

'They'll not be with us until Monday, so plenty of time to make some locker space, hehe.' He framed this like a joke but it was in fact a necessity; there simply weren't enough lockers.

'I ain't sharing my locker with no one.' said Linda, cheers rising around her. Was she really as stupid as she purported to be?

'Well, we'll cross that bridge when we come to it, hehe.' said Paul.

'How many of them are there?' cried Dean, frenzied little chimp.

'Uh, well, I've been running a new, sorry, *head office* have been running a new recruitment programme, so, uh, hehe.'

He was floundering and looked to me for guidance. *I won't help you,* I thought. *I hate you.*

'We're probably looking at, roughly, ooh, about twenty new starters.'

This provoked a spasm of outrage.

'Twenty?' cried Salman. 'That's like, double the staff we've got now.'

'Why is this *happening*?' screamed Dean, physically pulling his hair out. Linda, meanwhile, remained uncharacteristically quiet. She stared at Paul, then at me, her hair scraped back like tethered bullskin.

Paul was mauled by their illiterate questioning a while longer ('who'll pay for the biscuits?' 'How strong is a robot?'), eventually rescued by the necessity to open the store. 'Anything else, just ask,' he said. 'My door's always open.' This was an outright lie, his door was both closed *and* locked nearly all of the time. Those who knocked were kept waiting so long they inevitably gave up and sloped off to moan among themselves. I assumed this was a diversionary tactic, used to minimise contact with his verminous subordinates.

As the meeting adjourned I retreated to my office, curious about the details of the new intake. It seemed strange to hire such a flush of minions in a single stroke, I thought. I leafed through the pile, found Stephen Maltby's folder and flicked to his contract. It transpired he was being employed on a zero-hours contract, mitigating the necessity for paid holiday, redundancy and pension contributions. Also written into the contract was a dismissal clause whereby the company could sack him at a moment's notice. I leafed through the other nineteen employees and discovered they'd all signed the same document, an hourly, minimum wage agreement that could be terminated swiftly and without notice. I retrieved Linda's contract and compared it, noting the statutory holiday allowance, mandatory pension contributions, staff discount, notice period, right to appeal: all indisputable legalese amounting to a costlier and more safeguarded employee than the peasant slaves they'd recruited from the Scadmouth torture pit.

I ascertained that twenty salaried employees were soon to be joined by twenty desperate contractors with nominal workers' rights (might I be able to slap them?) on a significantly cheaper hourly rate. Was there something Paul wasn't telling me?

I arrived home that evening and slumped into bed, fatigued after an exhausting first week. The new employees' arrival had cast a shadow over my weekend – the admin involved would be *gruelling* – and I craved nothing besides a deep and enriching sleep. I was, however, distracted from such slumber by an itching in my ear. Was it a bedbug? Did they even exist? I scratched about and felt something light and crunchy on my pillow. Dismissing an eczematic episode as unlikely (I'd never been a sufferer), I examined the splintery dust that'd appeared on the pillow. It looked like shavings of some sort, light brown in colour, and I assumed a nearby termite's nest had been disturbed. I brushed the remainder off the pillow and dropped neatly into a snooze.

Monday brought with it a groundswell of chaos as the current workforce locked horns with the new intake. Paul was waiting at the door upon our arrival, welcoming us with an effusiveness that both chilled and unnerved. It appeared he'd been here all night, so pristine and twinkling was the produce. The staffroom had been hoovered and the microwave scrubbed of residual bean crust, utterly pointless given the calibre of the new joiners. I'd skimmed their CVs and could only imagine Peter Whamley's reaction. Given he'd described mine as a 'fookin' pile of shite', he'd have fallen off his chair to read these. (One of them had listed 'frogspawn collecting' as relevant experience.)

Once again we were assembled in the warehouse, split into two distinct sides with Paul hushing ineffectually in the middle. The room was fizzing. The new intake were fearful and jittery while Linda's side hissed like feral cats. Salman was whispering into Linda's ear and she nodded sternly. Once he'd finished she raised her voice and called for quiet.

'Hehe, thanks Linda,' said Paul. 'What would I do without you? Hehe.' It was clear he was deeply uncomfortable; his skin was spongy and his tongue darted out of his mouth like a baby frog's.

'So I just wanted to, hehe, introduce our new joiners, hehe.' At this he cast out his hand and displayed the new workers like a proud sex trafficker. 'Say hello, guys, come on, don't be shy.'

They mumbled vague, trembling pleasantries, the other side responding with ugly, indifferent snarls.

'I hope you'll make them feel welcome, show them around and whatnot, hehe.'

Linda stared at each new face, her puckish little mouth pursed and quizzical.

'Any questions?' said Paul, desperate for a quick wrap-up.

'I've got a question,' said Linda, making this as difficult as possible for him. 'Why are you taking on twenty new staff when it took six months to get the baler fixed? You told us there was nothing left in the budget.'

Paul removed his glasses and rubbed his eyes, an act of misdirection intended to invoke some compassion. *This is hard for me too*, it said.

'I think that's more of a one-to-one discussion, Linda,' he said. 'Maybe we can book in some time this week and go through it, just you and me. How does that sound? Hehehe.'

She shook her head. 'I think we should talk about it now,' she said. 'So we can all hear about it.'

While I detested Linda's fatuous guts, it pleased me immeasurably to see Paul so publicly humiliated. Far from the harmless dimwit I'd first encountered, he'd shown himself as both pernicious and cowardly, hopelessly invested in a company to whom he was nothing more than a cell on a spreadsheet.

'I really think this would be better as a one-to-one discussion Linda, hehe, let's get something in the diary, shall we? hehe.'

Evidently he'd been advised the most effective way of silencing a maggot was simply to repeat oneself *ad nauseaum*.

Linda persisted: 'and what about the Christmas party?' she said. 'We had to have that in the staffroom 'cause you said we couldn't afford a restaurant.'

I'd seen pictures of the Christmas party on the staff noticeboard. They'd been crammed into the staffroom and gifted a plastic bucket, half-filled with beer bottles, and a sorry selection of pork roll and off-brand monkey nuts.

'Hehe, hehe,' said Paul, shaken but resolute. 'As I've said, *twice* now, Linda, this is something we can discuss one-to-one, so let's put some time in the diary and talk about it then.' In lieu of an actual response he'd cunningly implied *she* was the one being unreasonable, his accountability seemingly forgotten in the face of such thuggish dissent.

She backed down and paced away, Salman in close pursuit. Paul put his glasses back on and tried to smile.

'Right, let's get your uniforms sorted, shall we? Hehe.'

CHAPTER 12

I sat before Paul's desk watching him spoon cheese curds into his mouth. He'd requested a breakfast meeting at which I'd incorrectly assumed breakfast would be provided. Thankfully I'd liberated an apricot from the market gutter so my stomach pain wasn't unbearable. The silence was broken only by the wet licking of his reptilian tongue as it lapped the foil lid.

'Hehe, sorry,' he said. 'I just like dairy. Have I told you that already?'

I said *yes* and hoped he'd choke on it.

'Something about it, I don't know. Just me, I guess, hehe.'

I said *mm-hmm* and remembered Peter Whamley's advice: *once you pass your probation you can spit in his face.*

'I need to ask you a favour,' he said, as if his orders were ever open for discussion. 'I've been writing up your new starter objectives.'

He handed me a sheet of paper. It was mostly corporate waffle I dismissed without bothering to read. One point, however, appeared more cryptic than the rest.

'What does this mean?' I said.

Oversee workforce exit strategy and facilitate all external appointments

Again he removed his glasses and rubbed his eyes, eliciting an involuntary flush of sympathy. I had to remind myself that I hated him.

'That's a tough one,' he said. 'Have you ever dismissed

anyone?'

I half-nodded, recalling trying to sack an ex-colleague and being marred by tedious employment law.

'You'll not have that problem here, hehe,' he said. 'Basically, your objective is to ensure the 'current crop', shall we say, are managed out effectively. Once the paperwork's taken care of you can authorise the dismissals and conduct the exit interviews. Does that make sense?'

I said *sort of* and he clarified: it was my contractual obligation to sack each and every staff member not on a zero-hours contract. Failure to do so would result in a failed probationary assessment, dismissal, and blacklisting by the company's myriad affiliates.

'How do I, what?' I said, goosing about my words, uncomprehending.

'It's easy,' he said, explaining how Dean had been stealing lapsed chops and selling them at underground meat exchanges.

'Breach of contract,' he said. 'That's him out the door.'

He'd printed a script I was to learn and repeat to every worker I was required to bin. It made liberal use of the phrases 'it's out of our hands', 'this comes from on high' and 'if it was up to me you'd stay' which were, of course, all lies, for Paul wielded a potent degree of autonomy and was free to make savings at his own discretion, reasoning the store's profitability would increase if all non-essential outgoings (pension contributions, sick pay) were slashed.

I returned to my office, dizzied by my new power. I passed Salman in the stockroom and he snickered under his breath. *I can't wait to sack you*, I thought.

∞

'Fookin' bastards,' boomed Peter Whamley, smashing his mug down. 'Fookin' slippery bunch of *bastards*.'

He'd called to check I was acclimatising to my new appointment and had lost his head when I told him about my role as workforce death reaper. I was now sitting in his office, mulching sticky white bread and gagging on Yorkshire Tea.

'I told you they were a slippery bunch of bastards,' he said. 'They got us on the fookin' fine print.'

We'd reviewed my contract and confirmed that I was, in fact, legally required to expedite all duties as requested by my manager.

'Looks like he's got you doing his dirty work.' he said, wedging more tea bags into his cup. The tea spilled onto the desk and his face grew puce. 'Fookin' slippery supermarket *bastards*.' he growled, turning to face the wall. His back turned, I nabbed a Jammie Dodger and slipped it into my pocket for later. There *is* such a thing as a free lunch, I thought.

'I knew they were recruiting but I didn't realise it was a total fookin' overhaul.'

'I know,' I said. 'How awful.'

'I didn't find 'em this new lot. They're fookin' phasing me out, going behind me back. Plus it doesn't make me look good if you don't pass your probation.'

I told him I was confident I'd pass but he shook his head.

'I wouldn't bet on it,' he said. 'Not with a cock's crawbag.' *More northern patois?*

His anxiety spooked me. He was concerned I'd been made a shill; a corporate fall guy enlisted solely to implement Paul's fiendish initiatives.

'Surely they'll not sack *me*,' I said. 'Who'd do all the admin? The holiday requests and the payroll stuff?'

'They're contractors ya twat,' he said. 'They're paid through an agency and they don't *get* any fookin' holiday.'

I was beginning to understand.

'You're fooked, basically.' he said.

∞

I lay in bed with my hair squeaking against the plastic in

which I'd wrapped my pillow. It'd rained all evening and the ceiling was leaking over my bedclothes; brown gutter water I feared I'd ingest during the night.

I'd noticed more unidentified shavings, this time on the floor by the front door, and was curious about the termite's nest. Where might you be hiding, little termites? The black mould would deter even the hardiest of rats, their feeble respiratory systems weak against the spore onslaught, so termites would surely stand no chance. Nevertheless I'd searched beneath the bed, behind the cooker and even outside the window, thrashing at the exterior wall with a sock in an effort to locate the nest, but found nothing.

I awoke the next day cold and saturated, the leak having been exacerbated by the night's downpour. I could only balk at what Gadswood might charge for this. Their bills were now appearing weekly, the latest of which included a 'seasonal decorative good faith contribution' which saw me charged for their office Christmas tree. Much like my contract of employment, these letters were torn up, wetted and used as extemporaneous wall stucco, a means by which to stem the ongoing structural damage.

As evidenced in these letters, and, more broadly, in their promotional literature, Gadswood lurked beneath a façade of propriety, relying on stock images of couples staring at hedges and client testimonials that were hilariously untrue. They claimed to have been certified by the GEAC, a regulatory body with a geometric logo and suspiciously gushing online reviews. The fine print revealed them to be the Gadswood's Estate Agents Committee, a subsidiary they'd founded solely to police themselves. Despite all the hallmarks of a legitimate operation, they remained happily unencumbered by any legal obligation to safeguard tenants' rights. Sheena had telephoned the GEAC's advice line when her kitchen sink was removed and replaced with an excavator bucket, incurring a reparation fee in addition to the standard grouting tariff. Having settled the payment, she was advised it was a water-saving initiative in keeping with environmental guidelines laid out by Parliament. The call ended with her failing to negotiate her way out of an overdue rent increase, an administrative oversight that'd cost Gadswood nearly one hundred pounds.

'Apparently they wouldn't have noticed if I'd kept my mouth shut.' she said, wisely neglecting to report maintenance issues ever again.

It was my fear of rent inflation that'd kept me from requesting a new windowpane, preferring instead to wrap myself in a sheet and hope pneumonia would gift me another spell in hospital. I consoled myself knowing such squalid conditions weren't inescapable, for I was planning to move once I'd saved enough money. Factoring in rent, fees, council tax, utilities and sustenance, I calculated I'd be out in approximately four years' time. This assumed I received my deposit back in full, kept my job and saw no increase in rent. Despite such woeful delusion I had no choice but to remain optimistic, my other option being to stab myself through the heart and get it over with. Unfortunately such mutilation remained prohibitively impractical, demonstrated by the 'fluids and solutions' fee Sheena had incurred after cutting her throat in a carpeted living area.

'They brought a chip and pin machine to the hospital,' she said. 'They said it was urgent they recouped the money.'

Her suicide bid had raised eyebrows at work, her spell of absence hotly debated among management. With no little magnanimity they'd agreed to grant her a day's sick leave, the rest being taken from her annual holiday allowance. Company guidelines suggested such unplanned absences were recorded as unpaid, a financial incontinuity she simply couldn't afford. With a cauterised jugular and one good lung she'd left the hospital and staggered to work where she was assured the deal was perfectly reasonable given the circumstances.

'Would you ask for time off for a hangover?' asked her line manager, defensive and stern.

She tried recalling the governmental guidelines she'd read on the subject but her head was cobwebbed with pain medication.

'Unfortunately they *are* just guidelines,' he said. 'Ultimately it comes down to company discretion I'm afraid.'

She was offered tepid words of sympathy before being reminded that this was a place of business and if the work didn't get done they all lost out.

'You see my dilemma?' he said, cleverly eliciting her sympathy. He paused.

'But I'm willing to meet you half way,' he said. 'How about you take the rest of the afternoon off?'

CHAPTER 13

Paul had requested I arrange a staff outing to a nearby pub, a manoeuvre intended to ease tensions between the factions and humanise the leadership team.

'They need to know we're not monsters, hehe.' he said, hoping to neutralise the redundancy backlash.

There'd been a budget of four hundred pounds allocated for the occasion, half of which Paul had returned to head office in an attempt to appear financially conscientious, leaving enough each for a drink and a packet of brine puffs. Despite the woeful underfunding Paul believed such an olive branch would help restore the morale shattered by the Christmas party.

'They need to know we haven't forgotten them,' he said, affecting a doleful tone. 'So many companies treat their staff badly these days.'

'Awful.' was all I could muster.

That afternoon I was required to visit the pub and ensure it catered for such parties. It was a bleak, neutered space, a low-ceilinged shithole smelling of disinfectant and fish pie. Sunlight sluiced through the grime, causing me to squint as dust particles danced before my eyes.

I sat at a sticky beechwood table, fidgeting as I awaited the manager's arrival. I'd hoped for a complimentary glug of Malbec but was advised this was against company policy and fobbed off with a poxy glass of pop. The décor recalled a bowling alley or low-budget hotel: shiny but oddly joyless, it'd been rinsed and lacquered so often the edges had been totally sanded away.

A man approached, chunky and squat. His cheeks drooped and his skin was cracked from a lifetime of insufficient sun protection.

'Sorry to keep you waiting mate,' he said, his pronunciation slovenly and thick. 'Been a mad morning.'

I eyed the pub's solitary customer; a weathered old drunk in a fisherman's hat for whom life simply couldn't get any worse.

'Pub trade's shit right now,' he said, clocking my grimace. 'Supermarket booze is killing us.' I nodded my concurrence, quietly wondering if the exorbitant price of a pint factored into the industry's accelerating failure.

'Too many people drinking at 'ome these days.' he said.

Thanks for the lecture, I thought, intrigued if wine priced at nine pounds a glass was contributing to his business's decline.

'I've tried everything,' he said. 'Open mic nights, quizzes, raffles, you name it. Nothing works.'

Despite his seniority he seemed utterly blind to his customers' needs, seemingly intent on ruining their evenings with amateur warbling and interrogative quiz questions.

'Anyway, that's for another time,' he said. 'What can I do for you mate?'

I outlined our requirements: a cordoned-off area wherein forty people could loiter and nibble nuts while pretending not to hate each other's guts. Could he arrange such an event?

'Absolutely mate, no worries.'

We dallied about the details and he took pages of notes, stopping abruptly when I made mention of the budget.

'You're looking at an 'undred quid for the booking,' he said. 'And I'll do you a deal on brine puffs. Fifty packets for forty quid?'

I agreed, assuming the salivating grunts would require sustenance. I was now left with sixty pounds with which to wrangle drinks.

'I'll do you a deal,' he said, as if he were somehow doing me a favour. 'Four bottles of red for sixty quid. And that's you robbing me.'

Once again I agreed, the piteous nature of the affair already exhausting. Four bottles of wine equated to 75ml per person, a serving the size of a small pet feeder.

'Sounds fine.' I said, handing over the cash.

∞

Budgetary constraints meant the drinks were scheduled for a Tuesday, the least noteworthy and most dispiriting of all days. I'd been required to plaster the staffroom with posters and advised by Paul that absenteeism would be frowned upon.

'Need to know who the team players are, hehe.' he said.

You're such a cretin, I thought.

Tacking up a poster I heard the door open behind me.

'What's that, a day out for posh twats?' said Linda, examining the notice. I explained that my living conditions were measurably worse than a kidnap victim's but she shook her head. 'Bet you live down a fuckin' goldmine.'

She noted the details and cocked her eyebrow, goblin-like. 'Free booze?' she said, her greed now whetted.

'Yes.' I said, overjoyed at the prospect of her disappointment. *Enjoy your thimbleful*, I thought.

'Might come along,' she said, hilariously unaware she'd be paying for her own drinks almost immediately. 'Might be a laugh.'

Yes I said, perfectly aware it wouldn't be a laugh.

'Be nice to see you without your uniform n'all.' she added, coquettishly popping a laxative into her mouth. Her hair was scraped back unusually tightly today, its tensile strength flexing her skin like industrial rubber.

'I'll be there.' I said, quickly hurrying from the room. Could I smell lust? She wasn't a handsome woman but nor was I much of a catch. I was both cash and asset poor, I had no friends and my parents were dead. My sister lived in the West Midlands with a husband who'd enjoyed a telephone affair with my ex-girlfriend and I'd become emaciated after being ravaged by housing poverty. If she wanted a meal ticket I was woefully ill equipped.

I returned to my office peculiarly flustered. The notion of sexual contact had unnerved me and my masculinity had withered at the thought. My last sexual encounter had been a sozzled tryst with a work colleague, a sandy-haired tyrant who'd later discredited my performance and ditched me for the testicles of a bulldogged shithead.

Linda was an altogether more daunting prospect. She was pernicious and scheming, a strategist whose stupidity only strengthened her position. Her knowledge of the store was peerless and it seemed she'd familiarised herself with every procedural tenet it was possible to know.

'She's going to be a tricky one,' said Paul. 'Maybe save her till last, see if she goes of her own accord.' The plan was to dismiss everyone she trusted, break her spirit and then hope she'd find employment elsewhere, forcing her hand and negating the need for redundancy pay.

'She'd cost us a bomb, hehe,' said Paul. 'All those years of work, can you imagine?'

He laughed, the yoghurt quivering on his tongue. How pathetic a person must be to bestow upon a company such unquestioning faith, I thought, scanning his desk. Eschewing photographs of his family he'd instead displayed pictures of himself, posing with corporate luminaries: the CFO, the Procurement Director, the head of Investor Relations, all grinning like they were celebrities and not corpulent slavedrivers.

'Have you booked the pub?' he asked, his breath creamy and warm.

Yes I said, outlining the details.

'Is four bottles a bit much?' he said, clocking the wine allowance. 'Any way we can cut that down? Put the money to better use?'

I said I'd phone the pub and amend the order, fascinated by his rampant inhumanity.

'Great,' he said. 'We don't want to encourage bad habits, hehe.' He scanned the order again, then a third time. 'Any dairy on the menu?' he said, more than a little perturbed.

No, I said, but I'd certainly request some.

'Hehe, thanks,' he said. 'I just like dairy.'

∞

The bar manager begrudgingly amended my order, bemoaning the decline of British pub culture under his breath. He mentioned that Tuesday was cocktail night, a gimmick intended to attract a more discerning class of punter.

'It's a tough gig though,' he said. 'Too many people drinking at 'ome these days.'

The cocktails, it transpired, cost twelve pounds and were served in 200ml champagne flutes. 'I just don't get why it's not more popular,' he said. 'Our barman went on a mixology course.'

'Mystifying,' I said. 'Do you do dairy?'

He offered me either yoghurts or cheese rinds, the former of which had been left unrefrigerated after a power failure.

'They'll do.' I said, hoping Paul would die of food poisoning.

∞

Having finished postering I was at something of a loose end. It'd been agreed I'd not sack anyone until after the drinks, a manoeuvre Paul believed would cultivate goodwill among the grunts: a proactive cushioning to absorb the heft of the fallout.

He'd scheduled a staff meeting whereby he'd explain

how the original budget hadn't been sufficient and he'd fought to have it increased. 'A little white lie,' he said. 'They need to know we're on their side, hehe.'

Such lies also laid the foundations for the impending redundancies, the implication being that cutbacks were imminent and sacrifices needed to be made. 'Two birds, one stone.' he said, his eyes darting excitedly.

I was thus left to fritter away the afternoon in a tiresome fug, my only task being to print name badges for the new contractors. I checked the holiday forms and noticed Salman had requested the day off immediately after the drinks. I marked it 'rejected' and tossed it aside, happy to have torpedoed such a blatant skive. Linda had requested the Christmas period off, ruefully conserving her days until the store's busiest period when she'd skulk off to Ramsgate or wherever the hell she came from. *Not this year*, I thought, rejecting it without a second thought. Doubtless she'd demand a meeting to discuss the issue but I'd leave that to Paul, his precision mawkishness more than a match for her idiocy. Her power lay in her troops; the oafish rabble she barked into a frenzy when it best served her needs, they who valued her years of experience as more than a chronic waste of time. Without them she was defenceless, a lone sow being led squealing to the slaughterhouse.

The clock struck four and I knocked off early, muttering about making some final arrangements with the pub when in fact I'd go home and catalogue my stolen teabags.

I returned to find Jasper talking to a group of tradesmen outside the front door. He seemed busy and was gesticulating cryptically with his hands. *Was he trying to extract money?* I slipped by unnoticed, ably avoiding a twenty-five pound doorstepping conference fee. I bolted upstairs and ripped open the envelope wedged beneath the door. It transpired I *had* been charged a doorstepping conference fee – I'd incurred it when we'd last passed on the stairs.

The room seemed different today. Something was subtly, intangibly out of place. Had Jasper let himself in? It wouldn't have been the first time. Not long after I'd arrived he'd used the spare key to access the property and remove all the lightbulbs, purportedly saving me money (*'light ain't cheap, bud'*) but for which I was charged a lumen reallocation fee of thirty-five pounds.

One evening I'd been awoken by Sheena thumping on my door; apparently she'd been burgled and her room vandalised. It later transpired Jasper had arrived for an inspection while she'd been at work, drank a bottle of vodka and smashed the place up, later billing her for the cleaning costs.

'It is what it is,' he'd said. 'Don't make a big thing of it, bud.'

Another evening she'd arrived home to find the landlord's mother-in-law boilwashing her hosiery on the gas hob. 'You might as well come back later,' she'd been told. 'I'll be here a while.'

She'd phoned Gadswood's and been told it was the tenant's obligation to allow the landlord reasonable use of the property during the rental period. Apparently this included sleeping facilities, food preparation and washing areas. 'It's all in your contract.' they'd helpfully confirmed.

Thankfully I'd avoided such intrusions, my bedsit clearly unsuitable for the scrubbing of familial undercrackers. Tonight, however, the room was disquieted, weighed with the intangible gnaw of something amiss. I quickly realised it was the straight lines that'd unseated me. My bed was flatter against the wall and the fishtank now stood flush against the cupboard. Examining this newly perpendicular arrangement I noticed small yet unmistakable pencil marks appearing at measured intervals along the wall. Tracing a line with my finger I followed them upwards, across the ceiling and down the adjacent wall, ending abruptly at the skirting board. My contemplation was interrupted by a rapping at the door.

'Hiya,' said Sheena, a popsock on her head. 'Have you got any teabags?'

Begrudgingly I gifted her a teabag and hoped she'd go away.

'Boilwashing,' she said, gesturing to her door. Inside I could see the landlord's mother-in-law hunched over the sink. 'She wanted advocaat but I didn't have any.'

I rolled my eyes and Sheena continued, 'she's here every week now. She keeps soiled nappies in her handbag.'

Crumbs, I said, wondering if it was okay to slam the door in her face.

She paused, slowly leaning towards me. 'I'm going to leave the gas on tonight,' she said. 'Just so you know.'

I looked at her, vaguely disapproving.

'If it happens, it happens,' she said, winking conspiratorially. 'Thanks for the teabag.'

That night I didn't sleep, fitful over Sheena's suicide. Gadswood would see to it her family were invoiced for the unpaid rent, plus I assumed there existed a cadaver transit fee chargeable in the event of death. I deliberated knocking on her door but was roused by a tapping at my own, relieved to have a reason to get up.

'Hi again,' said Sheena, an asthma inhaler in one hand. 'Just to let you know I've turned the gas off.'

'Oh good.' I said.

'It was starting to give me grief. In my lung, like.' She gestured to her chest and I nodded. 'Maybe another time,' she said. 'When it's warmer outside.'

I returned to bed, saddened it was Sheena and not Jasper who craved death, for if that were the case I'd happily seal his house shut and pipe in an external gas supply. I wasn't religious, per se, but I imagined there existed somewhere a deeper, darker hell, a distant purgatory to which lettings agents returned when their work on earth was done.

CHAPTER 14

Tuesday arrived with unprecedented gaiety. Miraculously it seemed Paul had succeeded in both raising morale *and* uniting the workforce, with the atmosphere uncharacteristically jovial. Dean skittered about the stockroom with a Santa hat on, barking dementedly at colleagues to 'drink, drink, drink!' in a foreshadowing of the evening's carnage. Salman jokingly told the new contractors he'd spike them and sell them into prostitution (*I'd do them a group discount.*), eliciting meek and fearful titters.

Today also marked Stephen Maltby's first day in the store. He'd ignored his official start date, advising he'd start 'when the spindle stops.' Not wanting to anger him I'd said this was fine, thinking little more about it. He'd arrived in a cagoule with a baseball hat pulled over his eyes.

'I'm here now,' he'd said, prompting Linda to recoil. She'd phoned me from the service desk and requested I call the police but he'd disappeared. He reappeared at the office door with his palm pressed against the glass.

'It's me again, isn't it?' he said when I opened it.

Yes, I said, petrified.

When I invited him to sit down he closed his eyes. 'It's a no from me.' he said, oddly shamanic.

Still standing, I gave him his contract, name badge and welcome brochure, all of which he bundled into a knapsack fastened around his waist. 'I've got it all now,' he said.

I was also required to issue him a uniform, an ordeal he didn't seem to mind. 'Hello little garments,' he hissed, yanking off his cagoule. He took the shirt with a trembling fist and hauled it over his torso, his head thrusting around inside as he found the neck hole. He stared into the mirror for a full minute before I interrupted by gently patting his arm.

'Let's go and meet Paul,' I said, keen to be rid of him. 'He's the store manager.'

I led him to Paul's office and could feel his breath, hot and sticky, on the back of my neck. He was tailing me so closely his shoes were clipping my heels, causing my pace to quicken instinctively. Paul's door was closed and we skulked outside like sex tourists, both listening to the faint clicking of a plastic spoon. *Another yoghurt,* I thought.

'Be out in a minute.' called Paul. Stephen, evidently amused, opened and closed his mouth like a fish.

Paul emerged from his cave, his lips pale with dairy. 'Sorry guys, hehe,' he said. 'Just having my breakfast.'

Before I could introduce them Stephen had clamped his hand around Paul's fingers and was squeezing them like a dog toy. 'It's me,' he said.

Paul dithered and flicked out his tongue, looking to me for guidance. *I hope he kills you,* I thought, relishing Stephen's unflinching grasp.

'Hehe, hi there, hehe,' said Paul. 'I'm Paul, hehe.' His tongue darted outwards and in, ticking with pain and fear. 'I'm the store manager, hehe.'

Stephen released him and bowed slightly. 'Stephen.' he said.

Paul led him inside and I paced away, eager to spend the rest of the day doing absolutely nothing.

There was a flurry of staffroom activity at five o' clock; workers frantically pulling on their civvies while swilling unbranded rum, understandably eager to enjoy the evening's sanctioned bender. Dean's cries of 'drink, drink, drink!' chimed through the corridors and Salman chugged heartily from a beer can, intermittently spitting it in the faces of the frightened contractors. Stephen stood with his back to the group, staring eerily at a wall.

Paul appeared at the door. 'Are we ready to go?' he said.

Yes I said, examining him. In place of his cardigan was a waterproof hiking jacket, padded and fussy with zip toggles.

'I'll rally the troops, hehe.' he said.

He entered the staffroom, narrowly avoiding a soaking by Salman, and clapped meekly. 'Hello hello,' he said, hoping for calm but roundly ignored. He tried clapping again but was drowned out by the shrieking hoard. He tapped Linda on the shoulder. 'Do me a favour, would you?' he said, prompting her to crow over the din. Such emasculation seemed not to bother him, instead he considered her an asset, a conduit via which his orders could be communicated to the labouring peasants. She clearly relished the role, considering it just reward for her much vaunted years of service.

'I ain't got no fancy degree,' she'd said, implying I was an Oxford honours graduate. 'I come 'ere straight out of school.' Then for good measure: 'I ain't a posh twat like you.'

The room calmed and Paul's tongue flicked outwards like a cuckoo. 'Thanks Linda, hehe,' he said, visibly overheating in his ludicrous raincoat. 'I just wanted to say 'have a great time tonight' and try not to drink too much, hehe hehe.' His stuttered chortle suggested a joke but he meant every word. Yesterday he'd advised I keep an eye out for troublemakers – those who underperformed the next day due to beer ingestion.

'Best to weed them out early.' he said, zealous with power.

A scan of the room saw a clear and awkward division. The full-timers were already half-drunk, clearly intending on becoming irreparably so by the night's end. Conversely, the contractors remained sedate and joyless, huddled by the sink in a timid cluster. Their sad reticence suggested Paul had advised them against such rambunctiousness, reiterating how he could sack them at a moment's notice. Given their brief tenure of employment their disrespect for him was still embryonic, an untended seed that'd soon blossom into unsalvageable hatred.

'We've not got transport arranged so we'll need to make our own way there, hehe. Does everyone know where we're going?'

An indifferent shrug confirmed that yes, they'd find the pub. Their immediate dispersal also suggested no one wanted to be stuck in a cab with Paul.

∞

The complimentary wine was gone in an instant, one bottle gulped by Linda and Salman while the others were stuffed into her handbag. 'Take what you can get round 'ere.' she said, slurring and nasty.

Dean had reached an insufferable fever pitch, screaming about football and spilling lager in the brine puffs. 'You can still eat 'em!' he roared.

Stephen stared out of a window, his glance distant and calm. He clutched a pint of dark stout and his mouth opened and closed very slowly. Was he singing? He was the only one still wearing his orange uniform and was thus comically conspicuous among the sportswear and stonewashed denim. Occasionally he'd be engaged in conversation by a revelling drunk who'd soon back away, perplexed by his foreboding riddles. Earlier in the evening I'd attempted such chitchat, amiably enquiring whether he was enjoying himself. 'Joy will find me in the end.' he said, gently closing his eyes.

The pub was pungent with orange and cloves and a miniature barrel simmered with mulled wine. The windows had been frosted with snow spray and the ceiling beams entwined with fir.

Paul stood at the bar surrounded by sycophantic contractors, all of whom sought protection from the marauding full-timers. They sipped sparingly, not wishing to engage in activities that might earn them the sack. They eagerly offered to buy Paul drinks but his temperance saw him decline such offers, setting a precedent for an evening of glum sobriety.

Salman and Linda had claimed the far end of the bar and were smashing back shots of Alcomax, a spirit drink made with diluted cleaning fluid.

'That's fuckin' *rank*,' crowed Linda, one eyelid loose and drooping. 'Let's 'ave another one.' Salman whooped with delight, shrieking about how much of a devil she was. 'You're too *much*, Linda!' he cried.

The evening drew on, the two camps increasingly polarised as the Alcomax tightened its grip. I set my glass down and made another trip to the lav (my twelfth) to sit in a cubicle and stare at the floor. Despite his implied comradeship I was firmly under Paul's command and knew my behaviour was being thoroughly scrutinised. I couldn't drink myself senseless because he'd advised I set an example for the contractors, nor could I leave lest I appeared not to be a team player. I was stranded watching thugs drink drain cleaner.

I emerged from the lav to find Linda loitering outside with a bottle of sugared vodka.

'Alright posh boy?' she said, her eyelid limper than before. 'Fancy a suck on this?'

Free from Paul's line of sight I gulped it down and smacked my lips, gasping at its strength. 'Go on, 'ave another suck.' she said, ingloriously flirtatious.

I did as I was told, this time holding her gaze as I wolfed down the revolting pink fluid. It hit me immediately, my skin reddening at its potency.

'Why don't you finish what you started?' she said, tipping the rest of the bottle down my throat. I barely held my gag reflex; so insufferable was the burn.

'Paul's looking for you,' she said, pursing her tadpole lips. 'He'd better not find you like this, eh?'

I tried to say *I'm fine* but instead sluiced out garbled mouth sounds. *What had she given me?*

'How about I take you 'ome?'

I couldn't risk Paul's disapproval but nor did I want to go home with Linda.

She had on a sparkly rollnecked pullover that emphasised her angular head and terse, pasty features. Her skin was eggshell white and peppered with freckle nests while around her neck hung thin gold jewellery strings.

We stumbled back to the bar and Linda scanned the room. 'He's still looking for you,' she said, clocking Paul's gaze. 'He's sent one of the new lot to find you.'

Fuck, I thought.

'Follow me,' she said, retreating towards to bogs. 'There's a fire exit back 'ere.'

She booted open an unmarked door and we tumbled out into the car park, shrieking and mad. She ordered a taxi and we stood in the freezing cold, waiting.

"Ere, this'll warm you up.' she said, pulling a wine bottle from her handbag. 'Get that down you.'

I obeyed, chugging frantically as my head spun further off its axis. Linda remained stoic, sipping coyly before hectoring me into further glugs. The vodka had left me pathetically amenable and I'd bolted half the bottle by the time the cab arrived.

Once in the car she began thrumming my crotch with a flattened palm and tensed forearm, pausing only to stick her calloused little tongue up my nostril.

'I want to cover you in vinegar,' she hissed. 'And lick it all off.'

I hoped we were heading to her place as I wasn't prepared to see another tin of pork in vinegar go to waste. Might she have Sarson's?

She lived in a low-roofed box house on the Bullmarsh

estate; a daunting labyrinth of underpasses and concrete steps that averaged three suicides a month. The front door opened into the living room and she bundled me inside. The room was a fetid little deathpit in which an oily-haired woman watched television in the dark.

'That's Aunt Tasmin,' said Linda. 'She's got gallstones.' Aunt Tasmin's armskin billowed like whale blubber as she brought a fag to her lips. Linda then left the room to unclog her guts. 'Usually takes about twenty minutes,' said Aunt Tasmin. 'I'd sit down if I was you.'

Unable to focus, I asked her what she was watching.

'It's about puddings,' she said, her voice slack and hopeless. She was like Linda but desperately more weathered. Her hair was hideously crimped and she breathed like a rusty bellows. On the screen a chef piped icing onto a slimy trifle and I noticed her tongue protruding like a flatworm.

The carpet surrounding the sofa was grey with introdden fag ash and the bin oozed with bloodied tissues. Cleverly, Aunt Tasmin had her next cig lit well before the current one was extinguished, a preparatory measure ensuring an uninterrupted nicotine supply. She smoked Thrushman's Supers, a cheap and vicious brand that'd been outlawed in the UK after users complained of jaundice and muscular deterioration. She sucked them puckishly, cackling about an uncle who brought her a suitcase full whenever he returned from Alicante.

'Tight git makes me pay for 'em though,' she said, implying an unsavoury sexual exchange. 'Rotten old bastard.'

The lavatory flushed for the sixth time as Linda's strangled colon hosed out the Alcomax, the fecal spitting audible from the living room.

'Sounds like she's 'ad a few tonight,' said Aunt Tasmin, her voice wheezing and dry. 'What did you give 'er? Fackin' drain cleaner?'

I told her about the brine puffs and expired yoghurt ration.

'Thanks a fackin' bunch,' she said. 'Looks like I'll be pissin' in the bucket again tonight.'

She explained how Linda would often excrete her own body weight and black out on the toilet floor, leaving her no choice but to urinate in a nearby mop bucket.

'I done a shit in there once n'all,' she said. 'It was either that or the washing up bowl.'

My throat burned as the smoke polluted my airways and my breathing once again became constricted.

'Could I have a glass of water?' I asked, hoping she'd not mistake such a request as the pampered demands of the bourgeoisie.

'Kitchen's 'frou there.' she said, nodding into the darkness.

I stepped over her legs and recoiled at her yellow toenails. The kitchen was cramped and beige and the sink was filled with defrosting mince. I poured a glass of water and tried to regulate my breathing after the inhalation of Thrushman's smoke. I washed my hands and noted they used unbranded trade soap – the same as was provided at work. I assumed this to be a coincidence until I noticed the same scouring pads, washing up liquid, kitchen roll and teabags. Did Linda use the same wholesaler?

I returned to the living room and found Aunt Tasmin immersed in an empty fag packet.

'That's an interesting soap you use.' I said, the familiar smell of lavender and turnips on my fingers.

'She nicks it from work,' she said, nodding to the bathroom. 'Fackin' nicks everything. We got a cupboard full of stolen bog rolls in there.'

I laughed, thoroughly admiring of such a scheme. What might *I* be able to pinch?

Aunt Tasmin held up the fag packet she'd been fiddling with. 'Look at that,' she said. She'd folded it into an origami rat whose head moved when she waggled its tail. 'Looks like my fackin' ex-'usband,' she laughed. 'Ratty old git.'

I indulged her nonsense before returning to the noble subject of theft.

'What else does she bring home?' I lowered my voice. 'Does she steal groceries?'

'Sometimes,' she said. 'Mostly meat though. We 'ad to get a new freezer to keep all the meat she was nicking.'

'Meat?' I said.

'Yeah, meat. *Meat*. None of your rubbish either. I'm talking chops, shoulders, the good stuff.'

Astonished by Linda's brassnecked fortitude, all I could muster was *blimey*.

CHAPTER 15

As foretold, Linda had lain on the lavatory floor until morning, stirring only to expel phlegm and unclip her bra clasps. I'd taken the bed while Aunt Tasmin had dozed off with a dusting of fag ash on her bosom.

Linda's room was a trove of stolen consumables, from the face pastes on the dressing table to the tampons scattered around the bin – everything I recognised from the store supply catalogue. She mustn't have bought her own bleach in *years*, I thought, deeply envious. I resolved to begin stealing as soon as I'd passed my probation.

I awoke feeling dreadful. My head pulsed with dehydration as my appetent organs sucked precious moisture from my brain, causing me to cry out in pain.

Linda then flapped into the room, already dressed, and told me to get ready. 'Come on, get up,' she said. 'That prick gave me a fuckin' warning about my timekeeping.' Obviously Paul was attempting to sully her record in preparation for her sacking.

She screwed her face up. 'Tosser.' She looked sallower than usual, like her skull had been shrunk and her skin stained with mustard.

'What're you waitin' for?' she snapped. 'Get your fuckin' clothes on.'

I rose and gathered my uniform, my head screaming and my mouth salty. 'Sorry,' I said.

We arrived together and parted immediately upon entering the store. We'd shared an excruciating bus journey wherein she'd assured me that should I mention last night to anyone she'd have her cousin hospitalise me. 'He's a fuckin' psychopath,' she said. 'He broke an old woman's legs once. For a dare.'

I shut myself in my office and drank so much water I was sick. My face was flecked with cornflakes of dry skin that multiplied as I picked them. I tried lathering hair wax into my face but that only exacerbated the irritation and caused me further blotching.

The clock claimed it was half past eight, meaning I was required to work for another *ten hours* before I could reasonably leave the premises. I was gasping down a particularly aggressive retch when the door opened and Paul dithered in, fresh from the solitary pint he'd nursed so assiduously last night.

'Someone needs an Alka Seltzer, hehe,' he joked, evidently unfamiliar with such grinding torment.

I nodded and hoped he'd leave immediately. *Please leave me alone,* I thought. *Please leave me to die.*

Presumably out of spite he pulled up a chair and began talking about redundancies. It'd been decided Dean would be sacked first. His dismissal would be an easy win and would, as Paul put it, 'thin out the herd'. I felt little compassion at the thought, reasoning that bottom feeders like him belonged squarely on the scrapheap.

Currently in his early twenties, Dean lived in his parents' maisonette near the Drillfield roundabout and spent every penny he earned on lager, frequently clocking on with breath like rotten yeast.

He was thin and ratchety and his face was pimpled with creamy yellow pustules. I envisaged bursting them and was momentarily excited by the thought of the discharge coiling out like an emergent maggot.

Frustratingly I needed a reason to sack him and couldn't simply boot him out because it was the right thing to do. Must bureaucracy always prevail? Paul had advised he'd been stealing chops and selling them at underground meat exchanges but his schedule left him little time to investigate. Supposedly he'd pack the meat into binbags, stash them in front of the store and collect them on his way out. It was an admirably brazen strategy: they were piled in plain sight and remained undisturbed until he moved them, for nobody looked twice at an unmarked binbag.

After several failed attempts at ensnarement, Paul advised I wait in the car park and catch him in the act. With no access to a car I stood in a trolley corral and froze half to death in the evening sleet. Checking the time it seemed Dean was late to leave, a common occurrence given his appalling record of punctuality.

It was nearing closing time and Salman's blocky frame emerged from inside. Slouching through the flustered shoppers I dearly hoped he'd be mugged or even killed on his way home. All it'd take was a slipshod motorist and he'd be pulp; troweled across the tarmac like rusty red horseradish. Instead he lit a Thrushman's and swaggered out of view, spitting on Paul's car as he passed.

Dean appeared several minutes later, hunched and scrawny with his arms hanging lank at his sides. He wore a hoody over his uniform and had changed into trainers, presumably to play football or outrun riot police. He scampered to the bin store and lifted a bag, the weight of which caused his legs to bow like sprung twigs. I braced myself for the confrontation, envisioning squawks of defiance as I gleefully threatened him with prosecution.

To my surprise he suddenly burst into a run, flying across the car park with the binbag slung over his shoulder. He slowed briefly to spit on Paul's car before racing on, gangly and spry.

The reason for his haste was the awaiting bus, an infrequent and unreliable service that'd show up only once the driver had finished his afternoon pints. Were one to miss it there'd be an interminable wait during which fellow colleagues would mither about transport workers being overpaid ingrates who deserved a good slap. Dean joined several such gargoyles as they tramped onto the bus, flicking cig butts onto the pavement as they boarded.

Panicking, I shuffled on behind them and tried to remain circumspect, for outside the confines of the workplace they could abuse and berate me with impunity.

Dean sat amidst the throng, animatedly nattering and sucking from a lager tin he'd retrieved from the binbag. In my haste I'd neglected to formulate a plan, foolishly relying on instinct and intuition. It was likely he'd be on his way home, surely a path I couldn't follow, for what excuse was there for loitering near a roundabout at this hour? He plucked another lager from the bag and snapped it open. Had he stolen those too?

We approached the Drillfield roundabout and he showed no movement, instead doodling breasts on the condensation of the window. He must not be going home, I thought, as the bus rattled on through the darkness, gradually emptying of passengers as we neared the end of the route. Dean remained in his seat, scattering tobacco over the floor as he furiously rolled cigarettes. His friends had alighted at various points throughout the journey, some drunk on his stolen lager, others on whatever they kept in their handbags, leaving him to stare, alone, into the night time.

We reached Crumbford Rise, a suburban hellscape made famous by a local dinnerlady who'd murdered three sex tourists in a layby. Terrifyingly, the bus terminated here and a single passenger remained besides Dean and I: a thick-set hooligan whose bulldog tattoo suggested he'd beat me senseless without the slightest provocation.

Exiting the bus Dean spotted me immediately. 'Hey,' he said, clasping his binbag. 'What're you doing here?'
The hooligan had stopped too. Would I end up like the dinnerlady's victims?

'What're *you* doing here?' I said, grasping.

'Oh I get it,' he said, winking and gesturing to the binbag. 'Say no more.'

Unwilling to arouse suspicion, I remained quiet, following as he led the hooligan and I across a stretch of wasteground, past a derelict petrol station and over a dual carriageway.

'Not much further,' he said, swinging his arm wildly. 'Keep up!'

The hooligan growled and tightened his windbreaker. *Who are you?* I thought, too intimidated to ask.

We arrived at a flat-roofed pub on the outskirts of an industrial estate; somewhere depot workers could peacefully spend their beer coupons. The evening was silent and the darkness overbearing. Might I be sold into the slave trade?

'Follow me,' said Dean, leading us inside. It was a small, hopeless scum depository in which several of the patrons looked genuinely dead. Evidently an attempt had been made to rejuvenate the place by distressing the tables and providing board games but the whiff of misery pervaded it all.

The barman acknowledged us with a conspiratorial nod.

'We're good to go, lads,' said Dean, ushering us onwards.

The barman's gaze followed as we exited through a back door and down a murky flight of steps, stopping at a thick steel door.

'Let me do the talking,' said Dean, heaving it open. The hooligan growled something about immigration and I stayed quiet. Where on earth was I?

I understood as soon as we entered. Assuming I'd sought involvement in his racket, Dean had brought me to the illegal meat market at which he unloaded his spoils. It was a huge, dank basement where pig carcasses hung like masturbation suicides, swinging to the interminable hum of catering freezers.

Flushed men with neck rolls exchanged wads of banknotes and eyed me with suspicion, aggrieved at the presence of an outsider. Did they think me a documentary filmmaker? Dean nodded greetings left and right, cadging cigs with an endearing cheek. If I were to leave this place alive, it'd be with him. The hooligan had wandered off, still muttering about border regulations but momentarily roused by the waxy flesh.

'He's Linda's cousin,' said Dean. 'Total nutcase. Broke an old woman's legs once.'

'What's he doing here?' I asked.

'He's in the trade,' said Dean. 'He always comes with me, sort of like a partner.'

Relieved he was on our side but pleased to be rid of him, I followed Dean to a dark corner of the basement where, half buried in shadow and propped against a freezer, sat a huge, sweaty butcher. His head was shaven and had a union flag tattooed into it, alerting me to his rampant racism. He held a cigarette in each hand, alternating puffs as his arms grew tired, the ash dropping crisply into a nearby eggcup.

Dean knelt before him and murmured inaudibly. The butcher sucked his cig and exhaled, gifting me an expressionless, terrifying glare. Did he think *I* was for sale? Dean chattered on and the butcher listened in silence. Several minutes passed and the sweat was beading on my forehead. It was *sweltering* in here. Shouldn't meat be kept cold? With no little fondness I recalled my own luncheon meat, bobbing innocently about the fishtank, comforted by the gentle brush of the cabbage leaves.

Dean shook the butcher's enormous hand. His eager grin suggested some agreement had been reached. 'I've put in a good word,' he said. 'He says he'll talk to you.'

The butcher's stare, ominous and unnerving, remained on me, sizing me up as I quivered like porridge skin.

'Tell him what you can get,' urged Dean. 'Tell him about our supply.'

I stepped forward in the oppressive heat, kneeling as Dean had done. The butcher gave a nod and blew smoke in my face. What was I supposed to say? 'I can get you sausages,'

I stuttered, floundering completely.

His eyes darted toward Dean, evidently unimpressed.

'Anything you like,' I said. 'Pork and leek, Cumberland...'

Dean quickly hauled me back, mouthing apologies to the butcher. 'What are you *doing*?' he hissed. 'This guy doesn't fuck around with sausages. He's big time: lamb shoulders, premium tenderloin, not fucking *sausages*.'

The pressure of the situation led me to apologise to the butcher, clarifying that my sausage talk had merely been a jovial icebreaker. In fact I could get him anything he wanted, specifically lamb shoulders and premium tenderloin. He seemed pleased, shooting Dean a nod and blowing more smoke in my face. Our business concluded, we hurried back to the tattooed milieu.

'Nice one,' said Dean. 'You're in!'

I asked what, exactly, I was 'in'. He looked confused, a carcass's shadow half shielding his face.

'Isn't that why you're here?' he asked, a note of suspicion in his voice. 'To get into the meat game?'

Naturally I confirmed that yes, that was why I was here, for why else would I have followed him such a distance? Lying hard, I clarified that I'd meant *whom*, exactly, was I involved with.

'That's Bloodpig Tony,' he said. 'He's the top man around here.'

He spoke reverently about Bloodpig Tony, explaining how he'd ascended in the meat racket after eating his own wife (*'no one messed with him after that.'*) and had a vast network of supermarket staff on his payroll.

He patted a swinging rump. 'We're going to make a mint!' he whooped, hoisting the binbag over his shoulder. 'Follow me, I need to drop this lot off.'

'Is this all from work?' I said, prodding the binbag. It felt moist and squashy beneath my fingers.

'Course,' he said, bemused. 'Where else?'

He led me to a door at the back of the basement, rusty

93

and stained a gruesome brown. He rapped and waited. 'This is where we get our money.' he said, yanking his hair. The door scraped open to reveal another wheezing great thug (a lifetime of pork fat had rendered these men blubbery and unwell) to whom Dean handed the binbag.

'Lots of goodies in there!' he called, the door slamming shut in his face. 'Should get a bit for that little lot,' he said. 'I'm saving up for my own tartan.'

'How often do you come here?' I asked, my greed piqued. Might I one day have *my* own tartan?

'Every couple of weeks I guess,' he said. 'Once I've stockpiled enough chops.'

The door opened and Dean fizzed excitedly, playfully elbowing my gut.

Instead of lavishing us with cashnotes as expected, the thug motioned us into the room. Did Bloodpig Tony want to eat us too?

The room was stark and looked as if it'd been used for unregulated organ extraction. Bloodpig Tony sat against one wall with belly rolls spilling over his beltline. He nodded to the thug (*don't you ever speak, Bloodpig?*) who then punched Dean full in the face. He sprawled to the ground and blood rushed from his nose, quickly staining the linoleum. I watched as he was beaten, mauled and knifed, his head thumped against the floor and his kneecaps stamped on until they cracked like water biscuits.

Once immobilised, Bloodpig Tony leant over him and stubbed a cigarette out on his neck. 'You want to explain why you've been stealing from me?' he purred.

Dean glugged up a mouthful of blood. 'I don't know what you're talking about Bloodpig,' he said. 'I'd never steal from you!'

The thug booted him in the chest, calmly shattering his sternum.

'Don't bullshit me,' hissed Bloodpig Tony, lighting another cig. 'Every time you come here I'm down a few chops. How do you explain that?'

Dean spat out two teeth and gasped. 'Honestly Bloodpig,' he said. 'I'd never do that to you.'

Bloodpig Tony peered at me, eyelids drooping. 'Let's ask your friend,' he said. 'See what he thinks.'

I trembled, terrified of a pasting. Dean stared at me; blackened, pleading, desperate. *Please*, he mouthed. *Please help me.*

Bloodpig Tony leaned in close, perspiration moist on his skin. 'What do you think?' he said. 'Is he a thief?'

The thug was smoking a cig, idly knocking Dean's head against the floor. I hesitated, thoroughly compromised. The thug extinguished his cig in the bloody pool around Dean's mouth and lit another. Bloodpig Tony leaned in closer.

'Is he a thief?' he repeated, genuinely terrifying.

Obviously Dean *was* a thief, but I couldn't attest to that now, for it wasn't merely his job he'd lose if I did. What kind of masochist must he be to have stolen from a man like this?

'No, no, absolutely not,' I said. 'He'd never do anything like that.'

Bloodpig Tony growled and blew more smoke in my face. Dean was in tears of pain as the thug ground his boot into his kidneys.

'Okay,' said Bloodpig, returning to Dean. 'I'm going to let this go. But if I ever see you here again I'll pull your guts out myself. I mean that.'

Dean nodded, still crying. We were bundled out of the room and thumped past the swinging carcasses towards the exit. Linda's cousin was loitering near a freezer and followed us out, murmuring something about migrant encampments. We dashed through the pub, over the dual carriageway, past the petrol station and over the wasteground, stopping for breath only when we reached the bus stop.

'Are you alright?' I said, dubious of the bandage Dean had fashioned from chewing gum and hedge leaves.

95

'I'll live,' he said, bleeding and humiliated. 'Thanks for sticking up for me.' His eyes glassed over. 'I honestly thought they were going to kill me.'

'What were you doing?' I said. 'Stealing from *him?*'

'I didn't!' cawed Dean. 'Honestly, I don't know what he was talking about.'

We were then interrupted by Linda's cousin rummaging inside his windbreaker.

'Fackin' good haul tonight,' he said. 'Even better than last time.'

We stood, frozen, as he revealed a stash of chops hidden about his person: up his jumper, down his trousers, thrust up his back. 'Easy pickins'' he said.

I arrived home at 4am, having waited two hours for a bus back from Crumbford.

Dean had slept the entire journey, leaving me to exchange fractious pleasantries with Linda's cousin who, it transpired, had been stealing on each and every visit, breezily pocketing whatever took his fancy. 'Don't see why I should 'ave to pay for it.' he said, explaining how foreign pigs were undercutting hardworking British pigs.

CHAPTER 16

Dean called in sick the next day, explaining he'd 'had a fall' and required rest. Paul summoned me to his office for an update on the sacking, eager to begin the cull. I eased his door open, hoping he'd had a stroke, but was predictably disappointed. He was leafing through a folder, dispiritingly alive and well (perhaps dairy *did* keep you healthy?), a copy of Dean's contract open on his desk.

'Don't mind me,' he said, peeling the lid off a fifth probiotic yoghurt drink. 'Just having my breakfast, hehe.'

I'd not had time for breakfast having overslept after my dreadful night's sleep. My pillows had again been crisp with mysterious wood shavings and the mould had spread further towards the bed, rendering me incapacitated after a night inhaling fungal mycotoxins. I'd also received another bill from Gadswood's, this time requesting immediate payment of urgent delineation costs and the associated partition fees. Freezing and exhausted, I'd set it on fire, gleaning warmth from the soothing blaze.

'So did you, er, catch him at it? hehe,' said Paul. 'Catch him red-handed, did you?'

Yes I said, thinking only of my probation. Once my job was secure I'd reconsider my principles but for now I had to push on, knifing in the back anyone who required it.

Paul advised I draft a statement and ensured a watertight case before Dean returned, at which point I could despatch him quickly and cleanly.

'It'll be like pouring salt on a slug,' he said. 'Quick and

painless. It might even be fun, hehe.'

I retreated to my office and wrote up my findings, stirred by a curious sadness. He'd be dismissed without notice or pay on the grounds of gross misconduct, replaced by a contractor with fewer rights than a baked bean. Should I feel bad about that?

The paperwork was joyless and tiresome: mostly legal waffle tediously detailing workers' entitlements, their rights of appeal, redundancy settlements and so on. Dean's was a straightforward case of theft and would, in theory, be resolved without incident. Should he contest the issue I was to intimidate him with prosecution, threatening judicial action that'd bankrupt and ultimately ruin him. As hilarious as this all was, I was gnawed at by a baseless guilt, something I imagined firing squads experienced when tasked with a taxing execution.

I was required to stay conscious until the working day was over so I ventured to the kitchen for coffee, hoping there might be some leftover taurine fluid in the fridge. I was greeted by Linda and Salman snickering over a magazine in which poor people disclosed personal tragedies for money.

'Look who it is,' said Linda. 'Alright Porkchop?'

Salman guffawed and threw back his fat head. He wrinkled his nose and mouthed *Porkchop* at Linda, validation that the nickname was in fact hilarious.

I pleaded with the kettle to boil and release me from my torment. Once boiled, I considered throwing the scalding water in Linda's face, ideally scarring her for life. It'd please me immeasurably to see her skin burnt and blistered, bandages requiring an hourly change, a possible infection. Did dreams ever come true?

The kettle's plasticky click disrupted my reverie, hauling me back to reality.

'What you 'avin?' said Linda. 'Sausage tea?'

Again Salman was floored, incapacitated with laughter. *Good luck in the dole queue*, I thought, vowing to savage his reputation as best I could.

The morning gave way to a listless afternoon fog during which I contemplated the merits of suicide. How wonderful to sleep and never wake up, I thought. Debts waived, contract terminated, hunger vanquished, all for a few moments of pain. It seemed almost *too* easy.

I arrived home to another bill from Gadswood's, this time stressing the urgency of my settling the delineation costs and associated partition fees. Clueless as to what these might mean, I dunked the bill in the fishtank and plastered it over the window crack.

Predictably I slept terribly, my chest hissing like a hydraulic piston as the mould desecrated my respiratory system. Even Dean's imminent sacking failed to lift my spirits, instead blanketing me in a cold carpet of dread as I curled into a ball, closed my eyes and dreamt of having my teeth pulled out.

The next day should've been one of the happiest of my life. I'd finally deliver an honest, decent sacking and enjoy all the power therein. Instead I shuffled to work in the hope an oncoming lorry might deliver me from my imminent responsibility.

Dean sat opposite me, scratching his head as I bumbled through his dismissal with a degree of incompetence that astonished us both. I spun a cobweb of half-digested sentences that managed to convey the message in the frankest and ugliest terms: he'd been caught stealing and was now being sacked. Any questions?

He accepted the order without issue. His mouth was downturned, eel-like, throughout the exchange, wordlessly accepting of his punishment.

'...and you'll receive no redundancy pay,' I said. 'Do you understand?'

He stared out of the window and I wondered if he felt betrayed. We weren't exactly *friends* but I couldn't shake the feeling that I'd wronged him; somehow broken our trust by dismissing him so cruelly. *He probably deserves it*, I thought, with all the conviction of a tobacco lobbyist.

Besides stealing a packet of stewing steak and urinating on Paul's car, Dean left with little fuss. As advised, I'd explained that the decision had come from 'on high' and was 'out of my hands'; at one point even claiming that I wished it weren't so. At this he seemed comforted, proclaiming me a 'good bloke' and floating the idea of a post-work pint. Curiously unable to decline, I said I'd think about it.

Linda scowled at me in the staffroom but otherwise it'd gone smoothly.

Dean was gone.

Salman was next.

CHAPTER 17

As remuneration for my noble scything Paul had granted me the afternoon off, patting me on the back as I left his office.

'Great stuff,' he said. 'Told you it'd be fun, hehe.'
I laughed like a sad dustbin. It'd not been fun at all. It'd been a hollow and saddening experience akin to switching off Grandma's machine six months before the due date.

'You'll get into the swing of it,' he said, sensing my reticence. 'This time next week you'll be like a blimmin' undertaker, hehe.'
I left the store with my head bowed, stopping only to spit on Paul's car on the way to the bus stop.

The front door was open when I arrived home. Had Sheena run out of oxygen? Almost immediately a tradesman appeared with two Thrushman's in his mouth (weren't they illegal?) and a toolbelt around his gut. *You're disgusting,* I thought, wondering how many lagers he'd had today *(twenty? twenty-five?)* and trying not to catch his eye.

He was loading paint cans into a van and grunted as I passed. Was that for my benefit? I quickly grunted back, hoping he'd not go into details of the various races he hated.

'All done.' he said.
'Thanks.' I said, quietly hoping he'd have a road accident.

I hurried inside, closed the door and immediately tripped over his dust sheet, slamming my face into the bannister. It'd been left in the hall, creased and filthy, and smelt like sweaty insulation. Clutching my forehead I tottered up to the bedsit, eager for some dinner and a lie down. I'd secured an off-brand pork pie from Dean's abandoned locker and was eager to draw nutrients from its coagulated jelly.

I pushed open my door and blinked. Had the knock to the head affected my vision? It seemed my depth of field was askew: the far wall looked closer than usual, the bed more tightly boxed in, the oven was...where was the oven? I stepped inside and composed myself. There was no mistaking it, the room was definitely smaller. Roughly half the size in fact. I looked up at the ceiling; the earlier pencil lines were gone, covered by a new wall. A partition wall.

'Hey dude,' came a voice.

Jasper clapped me on the shoulder. He was uncharacteristically casual, collar open and tie loosened. A pencil rested behind his ear. 'Didn't think you'd be home so early, bud.' he said, almost imperceptibly ruffled. He quickly reverted to professionalism and smiled. His teeth were exquisite.

'Wanted to have this all finished for when you got home but you're back early. Oh well, come in anyway. What do you think? Looks great, huh?'

I stepped across the room.

'Where's the other half?' I said, tapping on the partition. It felt flimsy and light.

'Unit renovation,' he said. 'Congratulations dude, you're now living in a New Build.' he put his arm around my shoulder and led me around the tiny space. 'All the mod cons you're used to,' he said, rapping on the fishtank, 'but far less to maintain. How does that feel? Sounds like a win-win to me.'

'Will this affect my rent?' I said. For a moment I was flush with optimism; a smaller room would surely mean a discount.

'Afraid so, buddy,' he said. 'We've kept the costs down

as best we can but a lot of it's unavoidable.'

He unfurled a billing document listing what I owed.

'We tried contacting you about the partition fees dude,' he said. 'Now we gotta charge you a late payment fee. Sorry bud.'

Sure enough, a thirty-four pound surcharge had been added to the delineation costs and associated partition fees. I read down: labourer sustenance fees, planning permission, parking costs, screw and bolt allowance, it seemed never to end. My eyes alighted on a separate section in which my monthly rental payments now appeared to have increased by four hundred pounds. Sensing my tension, Jasper squeezed my shoulder.

'Don't worry bud,' he said. 'I really pushed back on this. They wanted to backdate it six months but guess what? I told them to go fuck themselves. Said you were a stand-up guy and you were good for it. Honestly put my neck on the line. And d'you wanna know the good news?' He beamed. 'They went for it. The rent increase doesn't kick in until next month. How's about that for a bit of good luck?'

His aftershave wafted up my nose, the ethanol sweet and disarming. I said *thank you* very quietly and felt his arms tightening around my shoulders. Were we cuddling? The human contact was intoxicating and I felt small and limp in his grasp.

I was roused by a *thump-thump-thump* from behind the partition; an uneven shuffling of feet that felt like it was in the same room, probably because it was in the same room.

'What's that?' I said.

'Oh of course, that's the best bit,' he said. 'Say hi to your new neighbour.'

He knocked lightly on the wall, causing it to wobble.

'Hey sweetie, you there?'

I heard a groan from the other side.

'Give us a knock if you're there babe!'

A tired tap signalled the presence of someone on the

other side. 'Hiya.' said Sheena.

'Gotta chip off now, dude,' said Jasper. 'We're cool, okay?'

'No no,' I said, trying vainly to protest. 'When did this happen? Who did this?'

He was already out of earshot. 'Catch you later bud!'

The room, or at least my half of it, was now the size of a train vestibule. The partition had been cut to shape and wedged in place, a crude trim of sealant keeping it secure.

I heard a hinge squeak and froze, staring at the space beneath the sink. The angle of the partition meant my cupboard of non-perishable treasures fell on her side.

'Sheena!' I said. 'Give me back my fucking eggs!'

The shuffling stopped and she went quiet. Was she pretending to sleep?

A knock at the door. I eased it open.

'Here you go,' she said, handing me the packet. She'd shaved her head and had a bandage around her hand. 'I kept them safe for you.'

'What happened to your hair?' I said.

'I got rid of it,' she said. 'Wasn't doing me any good.'

I assumed she'd tried killing herself with scissors but hadn't gone through with it. *Why not just jump in front of a bus?* I thought, relishing the thought of inconveniencing so many commuters. I envisaged them clawing at the windows, photographing her shattered corpse as proof of lateness.

'You knocked off early?' said Sheena, picking at her bandage.

'Yes,' I said. 'What've you done to your hand?'

'Griddle pan,' she said. 'At work.'

Quite how a community muckraker got hold of a griddle pan was a mystery. Perhaps she'd been made to fry the shareholders' bacon.

'You up to much?' she said.

I couldn't say *I'm bobbing for cabbage leaves* so I ummed and ahhed instead.

'Fancy a tea?'

I sensed no lust in her words, nor was I in her debt. What could she possibly want?

'Don't worry,' she said, 'if you're busy.'

'No no,' I said. 'Come in.'

She squeezed in and sat on the bed, still tugging at the bandage.

'What were you griddling?' I said.

'On Mondays I fry for the managers,' she said, pulling at a fraying thread. 'Overdosed on pain meds, fell over, hand in the pan, blah blah blah.'

She seemed utterly bored at the logistics of suicide, leading me to proffer my commuter/bus idea.

'That'd be nice,' she said, a smile needling her lips. 'Don't think I'm ready for that though. Too soon.'

We debated other methods. Was hanging out of the question?

'Got a bad back.' she said, providing no clarification whatsoever.

Cutting her windpipe? 'Couldn't afford the cleaning costs.' she said, previously stung by Gadwood's fluids and solutions fee.

'You could do it over the sink,' I said, trying vaguely to be constructive.

She shook her head. 'Splashback, grouting, it's a no-go.'

I sipped my tea and stared at the new wall.

'What happened to your room?' I said.

'Landlord's grandma,' she said. 'Needed a holiday home.'

That's *bleak*, I thought, imagining a holiday spend hobbling around a bedsit riddled with carpet lice.

'Rent's gone up as well,' she said. 'Another four hundred pounds a month.'

'Same.' I said, recalling a story Jasper had told me about a tenant who'd contested such an increase. (*'I bankrupted his whole family.'*)

'Going to need a fourth job,' she said. 'I heard there's

some openings at the old coal pit, breaking rocks and so on. Might be worth a look.'

That sounds like a good opportunity, I said, trying not to burst into tears.

∞

It was soon after Dean's sacking that the excrement began appearing. It came like a plague, turning up in lockers, lunchboxes, on the shop floor, and most frequently on Paul's car. It seemed he was required to wipe faeces from the windscreen every day, often leaving dark smears and damaging the wipers. The new intake were also targeted, frequently complaining of turds stuffed into their coat pockets and backpacks. Paul theorised it was retribution for Dean's dismissal and a backlash against the new staffing initiative.

'It's happening *every day*,' he said. 'Yesterday I found one the size of a butternut squash.'

He was glugging from a carton of milk so frantically it was running down his neck and soaking his collar. 'Where's it all coming from? Who's doing it?'

'I don't know.' I said.

'Linda and Salman,' he said. 'It has to be. Who else?'
I concurred. It was their type of scheme, probably cooked up during an Alcomax session wherein he fed her cigs as she blasted the toilet with faeces.

'This morning I found one that looked like a moss boulder.' he said.
Recalling my discussion with Aunt Tasmin about Linda's colon I concluded there was no way she could've birthed such sizable loads.

'It's Salman.' I said.

'How do you know?' he said, fussing with another milk carton.

'I just know.' I said. I couldn't admit to having been at Linda's house lest she make good on her threat to have her

106

cousin hospitalise me.

Paul squinted, fiddling with his glasses. 'Unfortunately that's not going to be enough,' he sighed. 'We need to catch him, you know. *Doing it.*'
He sounded hollow and tired and I reminded myself that under no circumstances must I pity him.

'I'll try.' I said.

It'd become such a problem that staff began phoning in sick, complaining of stomach cramps caused by ingesting fecal matter. Some – most notably the contractors – didn't receive sick pay and had no reason to lie about such ailments, but the full-timers, eager to skive at a moment's notice, seized the opportunity to catch up on their drinking. They were spotted, buoyant and healthy, in various Prawnmoor pubs, tanking lager and spitting brine puffs at each other.

Salman was absent for a week and half, claiming his intestines were like 'coiled snakes' and that he required uninterrupted bedrest. During this time the faeces stopped altogether and Paul's car was befouled only by routine splatters of phlegm, a correlation that served only to ratify my theory that Salman was the perpetrator.

A thumping great box of a man, he'd been hired as part of a corporate rehabilitation initiative that forced carefree young offenders into menial service positions. Evidence of sexual misconduct had forced him out of his last job (he claimed to have been doing 'finger exercises' at the time) and his recruitment consultant had recommended him for the scheme. Eager for a mention in the programme's promotional literature, Paul had awarded him a shopfloor position, publicly extolling the corrective benefits of unpacking frozen chips. He'd had his photograph taken with the HR Director and was featured in the internal magazine ('*Neglected Hero Given Second Chance*') as an example of corporate social responsibility.

Despite the plaudits, he exhibited frequent and alarming signs of psychopathy. He was callous, manipulative and remorseless, often seen taunting dogs and tipping over pushchairs in the carpark. He was, without question, the perfect foil for Linda's slattern-mouthed idiocy.

Upon his return to work I was awarded the demeaning task of tailing him and collecting evidence of his excretal subterfuge.

'Only if you don't mind, hehe.' said Paul, fully aware I had no choice in the matter.

The store was also crucially understaffed, meaning I was required to cover several shopfloor shifts and rub up against the filthy general public. It was thankless, demeaning labour made infinitely worse by the customers, most of whom seemed to think they were emperors shopping for gold. I remained as discourteous as possible at all times, scowling in disgust when questioned about the mustards. It was during a particularly tortuous afternoon shift that I utilised the fecal plague for my own ends.

'Excuse me, do you work here?' said the customer, a dour woman fingering a notepad.

I walked away and pretended I'd not heard. *Drop dead*, I thought.

'Excuse me, I asked you a question.'
I stopped.

'Do you work here?' she said, tapping a pen against her pad. 'Could you tell me where you keep the flaxseed oil?'

I didn't answer. Her mouth hung open in expectation. '*Well?*'

'I don't know,' I said. 'What's flaxseed oil?'

She exhaled. Clearly I was exhausting her. 'Never mind,' she said. 'I'll find it myself.'

'Okay,' I said, careful not to apologise. I turned to leave, hoping she'd lose a parent to a degenerative illness.

'Although,' she said, 'You really ought to know these things, don't you think? They should really have trained you properly.'

Fizzing with anger I stormed to the frozen aisle and

repeatedly punched a packet of peas. Several shoppers edged away, muttering *let's get home*, where they'd presumably write a cowardly online review of my conduct.

Having desecrated the petit pois I caught my reflection in the glass of the fridge door. My face was pocked with dead skin, symptomatic of dehydration and a woeful diet, but behind the reflection was something else, something dark and bulbous resting among the broccoli. I opened the fridge and examined it. It was a huge, glistening stool, pinched at one end and stumpy at the other. With a carrier bag over my hand I lifted it out, careful not to compromise its structural integrity. It felt warm inside the plastic and I resisted the urge to squeeze it like a tube of toothpaste, instead cruising the store in search of the woman with the notepad. I found her in the poultry aisle examining clip strips and tutting like a woodpecker. Much to my delight she'd set her basket down and was paying it no attention. I stole past, invisible in the bustle, and quickly unwrapped the turd. Unbagged and sticky, I tossed it into the basket without breaking my stride, turning into an adjacent aisle before she'd even noticed. The shriek that followed was glorious.

Her groceries – pitted olives, forcemeat, coconut sugar – had been caked in excrement, their labels obscured beneath blobby brown smears.

'What the *hell* is that?' she said, her pen tossed away in fright. Several customers turned to enjoy the disruption, most pretended it wasn't happening.

'Are you alright?' I said, almost laughing in her face.

'I want to see the manager.' she said.

'Okay.' I said. *Go to hell*, I thought.

Paul tried ameliorating her with gift vouchers and grovelling apologies but she left without a word. Immediately afterwards he called me to his office.

'This needs to stop,' he said, puffed with purpose. 'Imagine if she'd been a mystery shopper.'

'Imagine.' I said.

'We need Salman gone. Asap.'

Later that week the news arrived that in fact she *had* been a mystery shopper, a snivelling grass sent by head office to evaluate the new contractors. Paul was devastated. All his hard work tarnished in an instant.

'They're threatening us with temporary closure,' he said. 'They want health and safety reports, cleanliness assessments, sanitary records, this is going to take *weeks* to sort out.'

I shrugged my vague acknowledgement, interpreting 'temporary closure' as 'time off work'.

'You've got to catch Salman,' he said. 'I can't risk our reputation for a few bits of poo.'

I bristled at hearing a grown man use the word 'poo'. *You're so pathetic*, I thought.

Paul had now been pricked where it hurt. He'd once told me the store was his family, his solace, his comfort. 'It's all I've got.' he said.

I asked what his wife might think if she heard him talk like that, at which point he recalled the Scadmouth rail disaster and asked I leave the room.

The excrement sightings had lessened since the mystery shopper incident. Perhaps Salman knew he was being surveilled and decided he'd made his point. Regardless, the health and safety reports found no evidence of negligence and the store was awarded a 'good' rating, a relief to Paul after such searing humiliation.

I remained in pursuit of Salman. I hoped he'd fall into complacency and blurt out something incriminating but he remained tight-lipped for now. Alongside Linda, he continued addressing me as 'Porkchop' and taunting me about my imagined wealth. During one such roasting they even suggested I pay Aunt Tasmin's gas bill.

'Why not? You're fuckin' rolling in it,' said Linda. 'What did you 'ave for breakfast? Fuckin' diamonds on toast?'

I tried explaining that my kitchen hob was now concealed behind a partition wall and I'd subsisted on egg powder for the last three days.

'Fuckin' Fabergé egg powder.' she said.

Salman threw his head back and hooted. Linda narrowed her eyes and squeezed out a smile, her expression suggesting she'd bestowed the gift of laughter. Salman's uncontrollable guffawing caused him to spill his tea over the floor.

'Someone else can clean that up,' he said, tossing his mug in the sink. 'I've got shit to do.'

He winked at Linda as he left the room. 'See y'tomorrow,' she said, feckless wretch.

'What's your hurry?' she said as I rushed after him. 'Forget to feed the servants?'

I half-laughed, resolving to bankrupt her should I ever attain the requisite power.

Salman had disappeared. The lavatory was just flushed and I padded inside, noticing a small polythene bag tucked into the cistern. I lifted the lid to reveal a wad of them floating there. *This must be how he transports the turds*, I thought. I followed the trail of toilet water out of the bathroom, through the warehouse and out to the store entrance. Why might he be taking excrement *out* of the building?

I scanned the car park and noticed him nearly fifty feet away, smoking a cig beside Paul's car and peering about suspiciously.

'What are you up to?' said Paul. He'd appeared behind me and patted my arm. 'Checking the bus times? Hehe.'

I nodded at Salman.

'What's he doing to my car?' said Paul. Believing he was alone, Salman took the polythene bag from his pocket and squeezed out the excrement. It landed with a *splat* on the windscreen. He stubbed his cig out on the bonnet and swaggered off to the bus stop.

Paul's mouth hung open. 'Is that…'

We approached the car and examined the stool. The impact had flattened it and it lay atop the glass like a cow's tongue. Paul flapped and fussed and I revelled in his unhappiness, confident I'd never had such little respect for anyone in my entire life.

'How could he do such an awful thing?' he said.

'I don't know.' I said, laughing inside. *I hope he shits on your grave.*

He shambled back inside for a cloth and I thought it time to clock off. It was Friday and there was little more I could do today. Salman had been caught red-handed. I'd draft up the paperwork on Monday and have him sacked by lunchtime.

CHAPTER 18

I'd been paid which meant I now had more money than I'd had for eight months. I ignored Gadswood's requests for immediate payment of everything I owed (a list that now ran at tens of thousands), instead treating myself to an onion sack and ten kilos of rice. This would ensure that when I was once again crippled by destitution I'd at least have something filling to eat. The shopkeeper warned against my boiling the rice (*'you'll give yourself arsenic poisoning.'*), advising I soak it overnight to reduce any potential risk. I said I had nothing to live for and if I could kill myself simply by eating a bowl of rice I'd do it without a second thought.

I knocked on Sheena's door and she appeared with a bloody tissue stuck to her head.

'I need to use the hob.' I said, gesturing to my jumbo rice bag.

While I'd been lucky enough to keep the kettle on my side of the wall, she'd struck gold with the gas ring.

'Come in.' she said, utterly defeated. Should I ask after her health?

'Is everything okay?' I said, only vaguely interested.

'Not really,' she said. 'I got behind on my rent so Jasper invoked the solicitation clause in my contract.'

'What does that mean?' I said. Would they start harvesting her organs?

'It means they can sublet the property for business use without my consent.'

'What kind of business use?' I said.

'Well, I've just had a prostitute using my bed,' she said. 'I had to wait in the hall while she had sex with a councilman.'

I looked at the bed and noticed a discarded condom. It'd not been knotted and the semen dribbled out onto the bedsheet. 'They've just left,' she said. 'I've not had a chance to tidy up.'

I mentioned the arsenic poisoning and Sheena eagerly boiled a pan of water. I'd eaten plenty of rice in my time but always remained tediously unharmed. Might tonight be any different?

'We can only hope.' she said.

Neither of us died, nor did we even fall ill. Sheena suggested we undercook the rice next time as that might increase the potency. The shopkeeper had advised excess water would rinse the arsenic from the grains, reducing the risk of contamination by as much as eighty percent.

'There's your solution,' said Sheena, her eyes sparkling for the first time since we'd met. 'Don't use as much water.'

We sat in silence, drank tea and tossed frozen peas at the wall.

'How did it go at the coal pit?' I said. 'Any jobs going?'

She set her mug down. 'There were actually. They needed a junior granite breaker. Doesn't pay much but it might help with the rent situation.'

'What does a granite breaker do?' I said.

Her one lung wheezed as she laughed at me. 'Good one.' she said.

I flicked a pea at the ceiling. 'Any business happening here tomorrow I should know about?'

I emphasised the word 'business' in a way that suggested she didn't know exactly what I meant.

She eyed a sheet of paper taped to the wall. 'It's booked out for the prostitute between eleven and six, then in the evening the landlord's uncle's bringing round his mistress.

They might stay the night depending on how much he has to drink.'

'Where will you stay?' I said.

'There's a broom cupboard at work,' she said. 'My supervisor rents it out on a nightly basis, sort of like a hotel room. If I sell a couple of teeth I might have enough for a night's stay.'

I stared into my tea. It was tepid and gungy and limescale flakes had collected at the bottom.

'You could stay at mine if you like,' I said. 'Means you'd not have to sell the teeth just yet.'

She smiled very shyly. 'I really appreciate that,' she said. 'But it won't solve anything. What'll happen the next night? Or the night after that?'

She was right. The situation was hopeless. Even if she were to sleep at mine indefinitely she'd still be liable for the four hundred pounds they'd added to the rent she already couldn't afford. Even if she were to secure the job breaking granite at the coal pit she'd be too exhausted to carry out her muckraking duties, risking dismissal and immediate loss of earnings.

'I could see if there are any jobs going at the supermarket,' I said. 'They've just hired a load of new staff so I could ask if there are still vacancies. Would that be somewhere you'd want to work?'

She wheezed. 'Would I have to rake freezing mud over septic drainage fields?'

I shook my head.

'Sign me up.' she said.

∞

Later that evening the landlord's uncle and his mistress crashed into Sheena's room and proceeded to argue like bull sharks. It seemed the mistress was unhappy with the arrangement and demanded a firmer commitment, while he cited his wife's obesity as the obstacle to their

115

happiness, claiming she required constant observation and care.

'Why don't you stop feeding her all that fucking cake mix?' said the mistress. I glanced at Sheena and saw she was salivating.

'I've forgotten what cake mix tastes like.' she said, quietly lost in a dream.

They rowed for most of the night without resolve. The uncle claimed he'd receive a life insurance payout when his wife died and was thus required to stay faithful. The mistress refuted this, calling him a liar and a gobshite. The spat culminated with the chilling assertion that he was, in fact, feeding his wife to death, systematically overloading her heart until cardiac arrest shocked her straight to hell. It was the only way, he said, of extricating himself from the marriage while remaining financially secure.

'Lucky bitch.' said Sheena.

'The mistress?' I said.

'The wife.'

∞

I woke the next morning to Sheena thumping on her door.

'Come on, get out!' she said. 'I didn't agree to this!'

With no luck removing them she returned to my room with her cheeks ruddied. 'They've locked the fucking door,' she said. 'I can hear them inside.'

The partition wall wobbled and a man's voice arose.

'I need to get ready for work,' she said, panicked. 'If I'm late I'll miss all the decent granite.'

I suggested phoning Jasper but we both knew he didn't answer on weekends (or evenings, or holidays) and even if he did, the fee incurred would be debilitating.

'Can you imagine?' she said. 'I still owe them for the weathervane that blew down.'

She hammered on the partition wall and the voice went quiet.

'Can you hear me? Get the *fuck* out of there!'

We fell silent and listened. There was a shifting sound.

'Sounds like they're leaving.' I said, unconvinced.

In actual fact they *were* leaving, prompting Sheena to wait in the hallway to accost them. They appeared at the door like fallen aristocrats, honeymooners on hard times. The uncle wore a thin suit with tears at the shoulders, suggesting a man with little pride intact. He seemed to belong to a gentler age, a time when children chased hoops and tea swirled with rat's milk. The mistress, while younger, looked weathered, tired from years climbing bedsit stairs.

'You know you've made me late for work?' said Sheena.

The uncle ignored her and shuffled past. 'Come on, let's go.' he said, cradling the mistress's waist.

'I'm talking to you.' said Sheena, verging on an asthma attack.

They barged past like shysters being accosted by a film crew. Her rage ballooned as they failed to acknowledge her and disappeared down the stairs.

'What the fuck was that?' she said, frantically pulling at her bandage. 'Why wouldn't they talk to me?'

I said I didn't know but comforted her with fantasies of their deaths.

'I hope it's slow,' she said. 'Slow and humiliating.'

Inside lay the remnants of the night's argument: broken glass, bloodied sheets, cracks in the plaster, surely little that could pass as wear and tear.

Sheena was close to tears. 'What have they done?' she said, her voice trembling. 'How did this happen?'

I picked glass out of the sink and folded clothes in an effort to appear helpful. A tin of frankfurters had been hurled at the wall and lay oozing brine on the carpet.

'That was supposed to last two weeks,' she said. 'What am I going to do?'

With a resourcefulness that surprised even me, I picked up the tin and plugged the brine leak with a sock.

'Good as new.' I said

CHAPTER 19

I'd phoned Peter Whamley to ascertain how I'd get Sheena a job.

'Why don't you come in for a chat y'sneaky bastard?' he said. 'I've not seen your ugly mug for ages.'

'Couldn't you just tell me now?' I said.

He stood firm. *Come in, then we'll talk.*

The directions he gave me were unfamiliar. 'Have you moved offices?' I said.

'Had to downsize,' he said. 'Bastard landlord kicked us out.'

I sympathised, agreeing with his assertion that all landlords deserved a lifetime of intense physical torture.

'Put the fookin' rent up,' he said. 'I told him to get fooked.'

The new premises were a far cry from the chrome and hatstands he'd once commanded. It was near Crumbford Rise, not far from the illegal meat basement I'd attended with Dean. I pressed the intercom and Peter Whamley's voice choked from a rusty buzzer: 'come on up y'bastard.'

The building was plain and yellowing and wouldn't have been considered attractive even in its prime. It was a functional plaster block for businesses without hope or capital, built when paedophiles still ruled the airwaves. He shared the premises with a tech startup and an independent brewery, both worthless and ripe for bankruptcy. Incidentally the brewery's logo was a bulldog with teeth bared, a nod to the ale industry's closeted racism.

My steps echoed through the passages as I ascended the stairwell. It seemed empty. Were the brewers out protesting immigration law?

I knocked at the door and noticed it was now marked simply 'Whamley Recruitment'.

'What happened to Poorfig?' I said when he answered.

'Bastard fooked me over,' he said, somewhat predictably.

He ushered me inside. It was a striplit little dungeon with archive boxes piled up to the ceiling.

'Drink?' he said.

'Okay,' I said, hesitant at the thought of a five-bag brew.

He snapped off a lager can and tossed it over. 'Get that down yer.'

I cracked it open and the beer was viscous and warm.

'Them brewers spot me a few cans now and then,' he said, nodding to the bulldog on the tin. 'Good lads.'

Light chinked through a window trussed up with filthy venetian slats. A crack ran the length of the pane and ensured a steady, freezing draft.

'My fault, that,' he said. 'Chucked a fookin' tea caddy at it. Fook knows what the agent's gonna charge for it. Only been here a month and I already owe them two grand. Do you know what a seasonal entertainment subsidy is?'

'I think it's a sort of Christmas tip.' I said, sorry he'd fallen into Gadswood's clutches.

'Bastards can fookin' whistle for that.' He gulped his beer. 'Drink up.' he said.

The beer was revolting, like tepid sluice water that'd been perfumed with thistles.

'Good stuff, that,' he said, clocking my upturned nose. 'Yeasty.'

He sat behind a makeshift desk fashioned from archive bins and an upturned whiteboard.

'Not much to look at,' he said. 'But it's what's in here

that counts.' He gestured to his heart.

'Absolutely,' I said. Should I phone a psychiatrist?

His copy of *Silencing the Maggots: Arguments for Cruelty in Business* lay open on the desk, comforting in its familiarity.

'I wasn't going to lose hold of *that*,' he said. 'Best book in the fookin' world, that.'

I pitied him; the text was clearly a white rabbit designed to dupe middle managers into believing they were more than just bureaucratic pond life.

'Been re-reading it recently,' he said. 'Been going through a bit of a bad patch.' He opened the book and took a breath.

"*Like rats your staff will scratch and scurry without direction. Do not waste time on humane traps, find the weak link and pump them full of poison.*"

'Where *are* your staff?' I said, noting his solitude.

He popped another can. 'Had to let 'em go,' he said. 'Lost a few contracts, couldn't keep going the way I was.'

I asked if he still worked with the supermarket.

'Now and again,' he said. 'Most of the business went down the shitter after they got them contractors in. Didn't need me any more. Binned me like *that*.' he snapped his fingers.

That's a shame, I said.

He glugged his beer. 'Still, they can't take this away from me, can they? A few beers with a pal? That'll see me right.'

I hesitated. *Was he talking about me?* I considered our relationship little more than an exchange of services, him steeling me against the working world while I earned him a commission for turning up. Now, at his lowest, he considered me a friend. *Thanks for nothing*, I thought, wondering why I'd been shouldered with such a burden. It seemed my friends now numbered two, one suicidal and the other psychiatrically unhinged. *Would either of them live through the winter?*

I explained Sheena's situation and he sighed and

121

scribbled a few notes.

'I've got no sway with the supermarket anymore,' he said. 'I might be able to put a word in though, if she's really good. What does she do at the moment?'

'She breaks rocks at the coal pit,' I said. 'And she's a muckraker.'

He drew his palm over his face and exhaled. 'She sounds like a fookin' peach.' he said.

A pause.

'I got you a fookin' job though, didn't I?'

Despite his mental state he *had* secured me gainful employment, steering me through two interviews while providing invaluable contempt for the whole process. Might he do the same for Sheena?

'I'll give it a fookin' good go,' he said, snapping open another lager (had he been drinking all day?) and tossing one at me. 'Get her to come in. We'll get her registered, jazz up her CV, brush her hair, whatever the fook needs doing.'

This was encouraging. Less so was the bottle of Alcomax he lifted from a drawer.

'Y'ever tried this stuff?' he said, filling two Styrofoam cups. 'Cheap as fook, it is. Helps y'sleep as well.'

We toasted Sheena and flung back the drink. 'I'll fookin' do y'proud.' he said.

We proceeded to finish the bottle and Peter Whamley cradled his face, bemoaning his misfortune like an old scarecrow.

'That bastard Poorfig left, that's when it started going to shit,' he said. 'Fookin' *bastard* left me high and dry.'

'Why did he leave?' I said, cheeks burning from the Alcomax. The bottle warned of chemical burns if applied to the skin and I wondered if it was actually diluted cyanide.

'He had other stuff going on,' he said. 'Said he wanted a quiet life. What a boring bastard, eh?'

In the nineties Solomon Poorfig had been a civil

servant who'd helped ex-offenders return to work after spells of incarceration. During this time he realised there was little financial gain in helping the needy ('let them rot' became his mantra), whereas larger, private organisations paid handsomely for services they believed would increase profits. He soon founded Poorfig Recruitment and operated out of the family shed, conducting client meetings at a cafe in a nearby garden centre ('the oxygen helps my concentration.') in lieu of a conference room.

Ethically barren, he poached the convicts on his contact list and sent them for interviews as financiers, estate agents and advertising executives, regularly omitting vital details from their CVs and advising they tick 'no' when asked about a criminal record. ('They never check,' he said, quite rightly, as the employer generally took the recruiter at his word).

He made enough to upscale to a smarter office and afford training weekends featuring ziplines and brandy. One such event, billed as *Grey Gold: Exploiting the Elderly* took place in Plugwood Forest, a leafy retreat somewhere on the south coast. Peter Whamley was his cabinmate on this occasion, there to improve his salesmanship and learn how better to defraud the vulnerable.

Initially disquieted by his roommate's boorish temperament, Solomon chose to spend his free time in the common area mingling with delegates, most of whom wore shoes costing upwards of six hundred pounds a pair.

Striding back to the cabin after a particularly gripping seminar on pension scamming (*'Money for Old Rope'*), Peter Whamley caught up with him.

'Fookin' crackin' that.' he said, red-faced and working class.

'Oh hello,' said Solomon. 'You enjoyed the session?'

'Fookin' loved it,' said Whamley. 'Proper fired me up, that has. Fancy a beer?'

Solomon hesitated. Despite auspicious beginnings his business was now successful. Weren't people like this beneath him?

'Come on, y'bastard. Let's get stuck into that bar.'
Buoyed by the rush of the seminar, Solomon agreed, reasoning he had little to lose by humouring a gregarious northerner.

Ensconced in the visitor's centre, Whamley glugged pints as Solomon sipped an intimidating Shiraz.

'So candidates contact you,' Whamley rambled, 'asking for jobs?'

'Correct.' said Solomon.

'And companies contact you,' he said, 'asking for candidates?'

'Correct again.'

'So what do *you* do?' he said, swallowing his pint in one hit.

'I match one to the other.'

'And they *pay* you for that?' said Whamley, visibly incredulous.

'Yes they do.'
Whamley cast an eye over Solomon's manicured nails and gleaming tan.

'Fook me,' he said. 'I'm in the wrong business.'

'What do you do?' asked Solomon. He assumed it involved suet procurement or something similarly revolting.

'Sales,' said Whamley. 'Pharmaceuticals.'

Solomon wrinkled a lip. 'Are you a good salesman?'

'I can fookin' sell anything, pal. Market's fooked at the moment though, no one's buying door-to-door no more.'
Though he didn't care, Solomon apologised for the state of the marketplace and wished him well.

'How 'bout you find us a job?' said Whamley, counting his change. *Had he enough for more lager?* If not he'd need to break into his wife's pension pot.

'I'm not sure I'd have anything you'd be interested in.' said Solomon.
Whamley hummed to himself, a quizzical expression on

his face.

'You said companies contact you when they need candidates.' he said.

'Correct. We're on their recruitment database.'

'So what happens when they *don't* need candidates? What do you do then?'

Solomon paused, discomforted by the question. Surely all businesses had periods of inactivity?

'We contact candidates. Find out if they're looking for work.'

'Sounds tricky,' said Whamley. 'What about exclusivity deals? Lock 'em in, that's what I'd do. Make sure you're the only bastard getting their cash.'

Solomon sipped his wine. 'How might I do that?' he said, magnanimously indulging the commoner.

'Cold call. Sell it to 'em. Tell 'em you'll guarantee them the best fookin' candidates for the next five years. Get a retainer nailed down. Diversify your revenue streams.'

Whamley's effusiveness was infectious. Had Solomon underestimated him?

'Make up testimonials. Charge over the odds. Drive around in a fookin' Rolls Royce. Them fookers need to know you're the biggest bastard in town.'

Solomon found himself note-taking in his head.

'But that's just what I'd do.' Whamley said, closing like a fly trap. 'I'm sure you're fine on your own.'

He sipped his pint and looked out of the window. 'That's a nice tree.' he said.

Duly ensnared, Solomon quizzed Whamley on his suggestions.

'If you want me, write me a fookin' cheque.' he said.

You are a good salesman, thought Solomon, quickly ordering another round of drinks.

They spent the remainder of the weekend drafting a business plan with revenue projections running into the millions.

Work began as soon as they arrived home. With a

roster of prison labour they set about beating the recruitment industry into submission, striking exclusivity deals – small at first, then larger – with businesses from all corners of the marketplace. Peter Whamley's brutish sales technique bulldozed all in its path; a colossal thump in the faces of mild-mannered resource executives more accustomed to the practiced patter of business reps.

He used blackmail, intimidation, verbal abuse and physical threats in his pitches, rarely leaving without a written agreement of some kind. His cause was aided by latent sociopathy, an undiagnosed and terrifying condition that left him guiltless over his actions. The recipients, through awe or fear, never reported him, for like an abusive lover he maintained it was for their own good; so invested was he in sourcing them the right candidates he'd willingly sacrifice his reputation, his principles, everything.

Meanwhile Solomon hired a slew of cheap, desperate interns, all of who believed working for nothing was worth it for the experience, a fallacious lie used to keep them subservient and docile. Soon realising they'd never be given paid work, most of the interns tried leaving after a matter of months. At such a juncture Solomon put his arm around them, escorted them from the premises and took them to a member's bar. As they were wowed by the complimentary olives he'd confide in them that Something Big was happening; that he was about to sign the biggest contract of his career. Would they follow him on this adventure? Initially reluctant (*'I can't pay my rent, I can't clothe myself, blah blah, waffle waffle'*), they were placated when Solomon promised that'd all be irrelevant when he floated the company on the stockmarket. Did they know much about IPOs? At this point the intern, amenable after two bottled lagers, began feeling valued for the first time in months. Solomon divulged privileged information, office gossip and plans for the future: hugely lucrative investments that could only be accomplished with a team willing to sacrifice a year of their time. *One year*, he reiterated, is all it'd take. Then you can buy your dog a fucking sports car.

The beleaguered intern usually protested a while longer, bartering for travel expenses or 'pocket money', at which point Solomon opened his wallet and handed over whatever was inside. The sum was irrelevant, never more than twenty or thirty pounds, but the gesture accomplished two things. Firstly it provided them the pocket money they'd previously groused about, a quick and easy fix that convinced them their grievances were being addressed. More crucially, it convinced them that the CEO, the company's *founder*, no less, was prepared to hand over his last penny to make them stay. Maybe they *were* onto a good thing after all?

'There'll be a lot more where that came from,' he'd say, ballooning their heads with specious thoughts of fortune. 'We just need to hang in there a while longer.'

Compounding the offensive, he'd then advise they take the rest of the day off to see their friends, get drunk, whatever it took to relax.

'You've earned it.' he lied.

This cycle of discontent and placation continued until either the intern faced eviction or realised it was a ploy to keep them labouring for free. At such a point Solomon swept them away like rotten logs, drafting in more young shills hungry for work experience.

The employees I'd met at the previous office were salaried, Whamley said, but remunerated poorly.

'Don't want 'em getting too comfy,' he said. 'Little bastards'll bleed y'dry.'

By the time they'd found me Solomon was already a silent partner, spitting his time between here and Alsace, where he'd invested in a truffle field.

'Made a fookin' mint,' said Whamley, quite obviously bitter. 'Left me on me arse to run this place.'

The company floundered without Solomon's guiding hand. The interns scattered as Whamley's bullish management style left them bruised and demoralised, one even accusing him of throwing tea in her face. It transpired I was the last candidate he'd placed before having to downgrade premises and dismiss the workforce.

'Just me now,' he said, gulping his beer. 'One man band. Don't fookin' need 'em. Bunch of bastards.'

We sat in his shitheap of an office and finished our cans. Rain gusted through the window and I was sure the draft would cause me windburn.

'Is there a radiator?' I said, anxious to thaw my brittle fingers.

'Pah!' he exclaimed, spitting Alcomax on the whiteboard. 'This ain't Buckingham Palace y'cheeky bastard.'

Evening had descended and the striplights glowed a fluorescent blue. I was drunk but cognisant. Peter Whamley was hammered.

'I'm a fookin' good recruiter,' he said, repeating himself over and over again. 'Fookin' brilliant recruiter, me...'

'I need to leave.' I said, swilling the last of the disgusting lager.

'Where the fook are you going?' he said. 'You can't get anywhere from here.'

'I'm going to the bus stop.' I said, fear jabbing at my guts.

'Buses have stopped, pal,' he said. 'Stop early at weekends.'

The fear was warming in its urgency.

'No, what?' I said. 'How am I going to get home?'

'I dunno pal. Fookin' Concorde?'

He tipped the remainder of the Alcomax down his throat and tossed the bottle across the room. It smashed and carpeted the floor with glass.

'Don't panic y'bastard,' he said, scraping open a drawer. 'Got another bottle in here.'

I crumpled into a chair (*was this garden furniture?*) and took the bottle, reasoning that if I were drunk enough I'd not feel the cold. My throat stiffened at the brittle chemical taste but I kept it down. Whamley's head was nodding and it seemed he was falling asleep.

'Do you know what makes a good recruiter?' he said, snapping awake. 'Y'can't get this from a fookin' book.'
I wasn't interested; I needed him to be quiet so I could think of a way to get home. I had no money for a taxi and it was miles back to town.

'A good recruiter needs two things.' he said.
Drop dead, Whamley, I'm trying to think.
'Y'need a fookin' backbone, for starters.'

Could I *run* home? I was thin from malnutrition so would skip along quite lithely, although the last time I'd run was many years ago, from a shopkeeper who'd caught me stealing an off-brand vermouth.

'Most importantly you need the fookin' *faith*, man.'
I surveyed his office and resigned myself to a night on the floor. It was dirty and busy with crumbs, presumably from the butter pies on which he subsisted.

'You've got to believe in your candidate like they're fookin' *God*.' he said.

There was a suit jacket on a hook behind the door; might I use that for warmth? It hung, limp and tired, on its fixture, purposeless since the client meetings had dried up.

'I had faith in you and what happened? You got a fookin' job. That's what I'm good at.'

I listened to him a while longer (more tosh about recruitment) before he fell into a sozzled slumber. His head rolled back and his mouth fell open revealing rows of fillings; little black dugouts between which festered beef rind and poppyseeds.

I covered myself with the jacket but felt no warmer. It smelt musty and cologned and the cuffs were dark with bloodstains. Had he recently cut his wrists?

Eventually I slid into a dream, thrashing in the shallows of unconsciousness, the icy draft keeping me from fully submerging.

I awoke to a blanket of blue light and rain spotting the window like urine. The blind slats were heavy with frost and icicles hung like nasal runoff. Peter Whamley sat behind his desk with his head squashed into his clavicle, his chin blubber providing ample cushioning for his sizeable jawbone. His mouth farted out strangled snorts and his hair bristled like a toilet brush. I squirmed as bolts of pain shot up my back. I needed to get out of here.

'Whamley,' I said, prodding his face. 'I'm going home. 'When do the buses start?'

He drooled gungy saliva onto the desk and peeled his eyes open.

'Bastard keeper...' he said, dreaming about football.

How awful it must be in your head, I thought.

'I'll make sure Sheena comes round in the week,' I said. 'Please try and get her a job.'

He was awake now, slobbily thumbing mucus from his eyes.

'Let's have a fookin' brew first,' he said. 'Get that bastard kettle on before I die of thirst.'

I prepared him a five-bag brew, supposedly his chosen strength on a day like today.

'Chuck another one in there y'stingy bastard,' he said. 'Feeling like a fookin' cabbagehead this morning.'

He was clearly unhinged. *Six* tea bags?

The room had lightened and we drank in silence. I stared at the rain and dreaded the return journey. It was twenty minutes to the bus stop and God knows how long before a bus arrived. The drivers' union had recently struck over a proposed alcohol ban during working hours – supposedly a nanny state initiative advocated by penpushers who valued procedure over humanity – and were only now reaching an agreement (three pints per shift, taken at rest stops, was the offer). This compromised the timetable and rendered it wildly inaccurate, often leaving passengers stranded for hours at a time, an especially terrifying prospect in Crumbford Rise.

Apparently even *toddlers* were mugged here, their dummies melted down to make breast implants for black market surgery.

'Do you know when the buses start?' I repeated. 'I really need to get home.'

'Dunno pal. Midday? Who knows.'

Thanks for nothing, I thought.

He flung the remaining tea down his throat and clicked the kettle on.

'Need another brew,' he said. 'One ain't enough for me in the mornings. You having another?'

I said *no, I'm fine thanks*, and emptied my mug into the sink. He crammed in another six tea bags and idly banged his fist against the wall.

'So this lass you were telling me about, what does she do again?'

I repeated Sheena's woeful credentials and he nodded his glum assent.

'Oh aye, that's right, I remember,' he said. 'She'll be a tough nut to crack. Can she use a computer?'

'I don't think so.'

'Don't matter,' he said. 'We'll embellish. Anyone can use a fookin' computer. Can she use a coffee machine?'

'I don't know,' I said. 'Probably not.'

'Don't worry, I'll teach her. Any old bastard can use a coffee machine.'

The kettle boiled and he guzzled the tea like healing wine, foolishly convinced of its health-giving properties.

'Get her to come in this week. We'll get her registered and go from there.'

The journey home took four hours, a gloomy tableau of freezing bus stops, gridlocked A roads and concrete blocks being hurled from overpasses. A further half hour was spent waiting at a rest stop while the driver enjoyed his afternoon pints.

'Union guidelines.' he said, lighting a Thrushman's and leaving us in a layby.

CHAPTER 20

I found Sheena in the hallway, curled into a foetal ball beneath a covering of wet newspaper. Beside her sat an empty cup of rice she'd neglected to cook before eating, enticed by the promise of arsenic poisoning.

'Hi,' I said. 'Are you alright?'

She blinked her eyes open and squinted at me. 'Am I dead?' she said, her voice tremulously hopeful.

'No, I'm sorry,' I said. 'Why are you out here?'

She motioned to the door. 'Prostitute's in there till seven.'

I checked the time. 'That's another *three hours.*' I said, noting the wet thumping sounds. *How long had she been bonking?*

'Would you like a cup of tea?' I said. My pockets were heavy with teabags lifted from Whamley's office. *That's what you get for sleeping in,* I thought.

'Thanks,' she said. 'I've been drinking toilet water all day. Be good to get something warm in me.'

She hauled herself up and followed me inside, her breathing shallow and quick.

Why didn't she just steal from the market traders? Surely any shortfall in profit would help speed their liquidation and clear the way for a carvery or tuna merchants.

She took a seat on the bed and stared at the wall. Her eyes were yellow and her joints snapped when she moved. She was examining a sheet of newspaper I'd stuck to the wall in an attempt at damp proofing.

'Council Pledges Thirty-Five New Homes in Dockside Development,' she read. 'The new build, nicknamed 'The Pendulum', will feature underground parking, a gymnasium and views of Drillfield Quays. It's hoped it'll help those with an eye on the property ladder.'

'How much do they cost?' I said.

She scanned down the page. 'One bedroom units start at six hundred and ninety-five thousand pounds.'

I laughed, seal-like. For a deposit of even *half a percent* I'd need upwards of three thousand pounds, a ludicrous sum given I could barely afford slug pellets.

'Better start saving,' she said. She laughed but her eyes were tearful. She paused before asking, 'what'll happen to us?' Her voice had shrunk to a whisper. 'I mean, is this it for us? Do we just keep working until we're too old to work? What then? What happens when we can't afford the rent? Go and live in a garage?'

I neglected to mention that garages now cost upward of seventy thousand pounds, more if served by good transport links.

She continued: 'when I was at university I put away money every week. Not a lot, but I did it for four years. Every week without fail. Sometimes I'd even forego fags.'

I handed her the tea and tried to think of something encouraging to say. 'Wow,' I said. 'That's good.'

She stared at the milky fluid. 'I put it in a high interest account and didn't touch it for two years after I graduated. I wanted a kind of, nest egg, I suppose. Money on hand for when I set up on my own.'

Already sure of the answer, I asked if she had any of it left.

'What do you think?'

I shook my head. This obviously wasn't going to end well.

'Two months rent and it was gone. Lettings agent took it all.'

That's a shame, I said, vaguely sympathetic. 'What did you do?'

'I was going to move back to Wales but Mum and Dad

had been caught running a bloodfarm near Bridgend. I had nothing to go back to.'

'What's a bloodfarm?' I said, hoping to lighten the mood.

'It's where they extract horse blood,' she said. 'It contains a fertility hormone they inject into livestock to increase birth rates. Mum always used to say, 'more babies, more bacon!''

She repeated this mantra under her breath, pricked by love and revulsion. *More babies, more bacon! More babies, more bacon!*

'They got eight years for animal cruelty and breach of welfare regulations. The house got vandalised and Dad, bless him, he killed himself before they could lock him up. Threw himself off a fun slide. Mum's in prison but she won't have any visitors. Apparently she's sleeping with a torture murderer from Cowbridge.'

Crumbs, I thought. 'What about brothers and sisters?' I said, instinctively assuming the worst. 'Are they still around?'

'My brother died when he was sixteen,' she said (of *course* he did). 'Chased a sheepdog into a ravine. Slipped on a rock, drowned, died.'

I noticed a throb of petulance in her voice. Was she *jealous?*

'It's just me now. I've got a grandma in Cardiff but she's disowned our side of the family. She thinks we're cursed.'

'That's crazy,' I said, lying of course.

The prostitute had ceased thumping and we quietened to whispers. *Had she stopped for a breather?*

'Have you ever been with a prostitute?' asked Sheena.

I put my ear to the partition wall. 'No,' I said. 'Never had the money.'

This was absolutely true. My income had never enabled me to afford such luxuries. Should my salary ever exceed breadline levels I'd happily solicit such services, perhaps even schedule a monthly visit. I hauled myself out of my daydream and quickly regretted my capriciousness, for hope was less affordable than sexual satisfaction.

'Have you?' I said.

She stared at the wall and didn't answer. Several seconds passed in silence. 'Can we talk about something else?'

I fussed with a teaspoon, wondering how best to progress the discussion, for it seemed every avenue might end in tragedy.

'How did it go with the recruiter?' she said, helpfully changing tact.

'It went well.' I said. This, again, was a lie. Peter Whamley was a man without hope, a garrulous husk for whom alcoholic oblivion was the only attainable escape. 'He wants to meet you during the week.' I said.

It was then I saw her smile for the second time since we'd met: a thin, cautious glimmer that suggested there might yet be something to live for. *There isn't*, I thought, aware the only jobs she'd be qualified for involved scrubbing slime off boat hulls or fighting in the backrooms of pubs.

'Wow, thank you,' she said. 'I don't know what to say.'

I felt a stab of guilt as I absorbed her goodwill, a quick knock to the head reminding me that I might have actually aggravated things by helping postpone her suicide, for in heaven there were no middle managers, no performance reviews, no national insurance contributions. Had I robbed her of a chance at happiness?

I handed her one of his business cards. Beer had stained it a light brown.

'That's a bit of a trek,' she said, noting the address. 'Crumbford's miles away.'

I puffed my cheeks in terse agreement. 'Takes a good four hours, I said. 'There and back.'

'Hopefully I can dodge the bus fare,' she said. 'If I dislocate my shoulder they usually let me off.'

A door slammed and we heard a strutting from the staircase.

'Sounds like she's done for the day.' I said.

Sheena's head tipped backwards against the wall, resigned, exhausted.

'More semen to clean up,' she said, her moment of promise extinguished. 'Last week it was everywhere: streaked up the windows, in the sink, in my coffee mug - I can smell it on my pillow when I wake up.'

That's revolting I said, trying to determine whether I'd be aroused ejaculating into a basin.

CHAPTER 21

I'd slept terribly because I had to go to work tomorrow. I'd been so preoccupied with Sheena's misery I'd forgotten how much I hated it, and I hated it a *lot*. As the bus rolled past graveyards and sausage factories I ruminated on her deathwish and wondered how much longer *I* might live. Thirty years? Thirty-five at a push? How much of that would I waste in the back office of a supermarket?

If I succeeded in passing my probation I'd have secured a full-time job, a tortuous necessity that condemned me to a lifetime of interminable grunt work as I grew weak and matted and useless. If I failed I'd slip back into poverty, wheezing to death as I scrambled in the gutter for dog biscuits. Both outcomes were unthinkably bleak.

Today I'd been tasked with sacking Salman, ostensibly a straightforward task given what we'd caught him doing. To me he elicited nothing but hatred and disgust (my heart would soar to see him destitute and eating from dustbins), yet still I was intimidated. Besides his intense physical bulk (he was the size of four oil drums) his psychopathy rendered him both manipulative and unfazed by punitive measures.

(During the first month of his employment he'd lured a colleague to the delivery bay and talked them into a freezer truck where they'd stayed imprisoned for nearly an hour. Only after a series of cryptic riddles pinned to the staff noticeboard was a search mounted and the missing employee found, alive but freezing. When questioned,

Salman maintained they'd locked themselves in the truck to 'cool down' after a tiring shift. When asked why the door had been locked from the outside he shrugged, nonchalantly claiming 'I'm not a fucking locksmith.'

The colleague spent a month in hospital with frostbite and pneumonia, a gruelling spell during which a toy snowman was delivered, anonymously, to the ward. There was no identifiable sender but it came packaged with cooking instructions for frozen beef burgers. Seeing this, the victim yanked out their IV drips and bolted from the room screaming 'don't eat me', until forcibly sedated.)

Paul had requested a preparatory meeting to discuss the disposal of such a monster. He sat at his desk, zipped into a sports fleece (*so* pathetic), eating a custard tart.

'So today's the big day, hehe,' he said. His words were rapid and clipped. 'Tell you what, Dean was an easy win. This guy's a different story, hehe.'

He seemed nervous on my behalf, sneering coward.

'Is everything alright?' I said, hoping he was on the cusp of a breakdown.

He rubbed his nose and sighed, pensive as his bulbous eyes narrowed behind his glasses. Despite his odiousness, or perhaps because of it, he was able to elicit an uncanny degree of sympathy, a trick he employed whenever the discussion forked into the realms of discomfort.

He bit off some custard tart and chewed with nervous jerks.

'He was a charity hire,' he said. 'We had some great press for getting him through the door, I'll tell you that. I even got invited to a fundraising dinner.' He squeezed his eyes shut as if pained by the memory. 'Best night of my life.' he said.

What might his criteria for a great night be? It'd almost certainly involve dairy, perhaps a butter churn or clotted fountain (could you hire such things?) and subordinates over whom he could wield his lowly vestiges of power. Above all, however, it'd be recognition for his work;

confirmation he was a valued resource and not an expendable nobody whose death would trouble no one but the earthworms. (The emails he sent head office, some of which I'd seen, were unimaginably simpering. He'd recently asked me to proofread a six-paragraph missive on the versatility of wire dump bins he wrote during a 'lightbulb moment' in the middle of the night.)

'Is he in today, hehe?' he said, nibbling the tart crust.

I checked the rota. 'He should be.' I said.

We both knew this was no guarantee of Salman's attendance. If he didn't fancy turning up we'd hear of it only if Linda bothered relaying the message.

'He's going to be a nasty one, I can tell,' said Paul. 'God knows what we'll do if he won't go.' His tongue darted out to catch a custard morsel. 'But we'll not worry about that just yet, hehe. Just get him in a room first.'

I left him picking crumbs from the desk with a wet fingertip. Might I ever plumb such depths?

I combed the store without success. Salman either hadn't arrived or was taking the day off to dissect living creatures and draw strength from their screams.

'Why you sniffing about out 'ere Porkchop?' Linda had clocked me scanning the aisles and sensed something was up. 'You lost your fuckin' crown or something?'

Did she honestly think me a *king*?

'I'm looking for Salman,' I said. 'Do you know if he's in today?'

She peered directly into my brain. Her eyes were pale and beige, creased from years spent frowning.

'Why, you gonna sack him n'all?'

'No, absolutely not.' I said, lying beautifully.

'He'll be in later,' she said. 'He's clippin' his toenails.'

The contempt was extraordinary. They hated me, of course, but I was merely a conduit. Their disrespect for Paul was so prodigious they didn't bother even *pretending* to lie convincingly.

'Oh right,' I said. 'Thanks.'

Without knowing his whereabouts I was unable to prepare adequately for the confrontation. I'd asked Linda to send him in when he arrived but it was doubtful she'd bother, for it seemed she'd resolved to make things as difficult for me as she possibly could.

'If you don't like it, go back to fuckin' Cambridge.' she'd said.

I rejected more of Linda's holiday requests but even that failed to relax me. I paced the office, rereading Paul's notes and letting the words percolate in my mouth. The door squeaked behind me and I barked in fright.

'Only me, hehe,' said Paul. 'Someone's a bit jumpy!'

Go to hell, I thought.

'Any sign of him yet?' he said, unscrewing a probiotic drink. He gulped it in one breath and wiped yellow dribble from his chin.

'He's clipping his toenails.' I said.

'Well, let me know when he gets here, hehe.' he said.

I hoped he'd leave me alone but he lingered like a recurring cyst.

'One more thing,' he said. 'Bit of a delicate matter actually, hehe. You wouldn't happen to know anyone who's, er, *disadvantaged* would you?'

What are you talking about, idiot?

'Since we're losing Salman we could do with employing someone from the, hehe, not quite sure how to put this, the 'untidy end of the sock drawer', if you know what I mean.'

Relishing his discomfort, I reassured him I had no idea what he was talking about.

He continued, now somewhat ruffled: 'maybe they've been in prison, maybe they've got one leg. Homeless even. Do you get what I mean?'

I sort-of nodded but remained consciously nonplussed.

'Something I can tell the HR Director about, something that'd look good in the magazine, you know?'

I said *I'll think about it* but would do nothing of the sort, warmly embracing anything that'd cause him even the slightest inconvenience.

'Thanks,' he said. 'Just putting the feelers out. It's a sensitive subject you know, hehe.'

At this moment he rubbed his temple in a show of martyred exhaustion, causing me a weird gnaw of pity I had to wilfully suppress.

'It's so hard keeping top brass happy.' he said.

Don't pity him, I thought.

Predictably Linda made no mention of Salman's arrival, instead I saw him disembarking the bus when I stepped out to spit on Paul's car. I was probably imagining it but his swagger seemed more buoyant today. Perhaps his toenails really had been clipped.

I scurried inside and flapped with papers and contracts, sweat pebbling on my forehead as the confrontation drew nearer. Soon I'd be close enough to smell his sweat, earthy and vinegary sweet.

Naturally I was thrilled at the idea of sacking such a verminous lump, my thoughts tumbling towards a bright future wherein his benefits were stopped and he was evicted onto the freezing streets, snapping at commuters for beer coins and soiling himself in doorways. While my heart soared to cradle such power, I was terrified he'd thump me, for without a job to cling to, what might stop him?

I heard heavy footsteps. He was coming. Glued to my seat I stared at the door and prepared to face him, my fingers grasping at the matted armrest. The stomping stopped outside and he peered in, his eyes blinking through the thin strip of glass. Like a restaurant lobster I wanted to scurry behind a rock lest I be torn apart and have my digestive gland eaten.

Instead of entering he disappeared. *Where are you going, scum?*

I heard a snigger. Should I chase him?

I heard the kettle click. He was making tea. This was

followed by rustling and muttered curses and I surmised he was rifling through the bin for teabags. In a new initiative seemingly designed to inconvenience the shopfloor grunts, Paul had cut all staffroom sundries from the store budget, meaning it fell to the workers to provide their own tea and coffee. Chaos ensued when they devised a turn-based rota system that was roundly ignored as they all refused to pay their share. Stephen Maltby claimed spraying fixative on a teabag increased its resilience and enabled three days' usage. 'I'm right about this.' he said, his voice lilting into song.

Linda, of course, suggested I pay for it, advising I sell one of my slaves to cover the cost. 'What about the one who cleans your ballsack?' she'd said, causing Salman to fall off his chair.

Paul feigned frustration throughout, claiming it was a cost saving measure that was out of his hands. Meanwhile he watched as they accused each other of stealing coffee whitener (that'd been me) and squabbled over sugar packets. Despite an increase in complaints and the occasional lunchbreak spent counselling tearful contractors, he seemed mostly unperturbed by the dissent.

'Let them fight,' he said. 'With any luck they'll kill each other, hehe.'

Salman hadn't yet come to the door. Despite my fractiousness I'd resolved to give him a last five minutes, for even death row inmates were granted a last meal, a privilege they usually squandered on fried chicken and ice cream. (Personally I'd request jellied salmon and tuna platelets, lightly dusted with onion power.)

I checked the time and rose, tucking folders under my arm in a bid to appear officious. He was lounging in the staffroom reading the sports pages and chuffing an electrofag. His shirt was untucked and his cheeks were tubby and pustuled. He was swilling tea around his mouth and gargling loudly as it cooled. *You're disgusting,* I thought.

'What do you want, Porkchop?' he said, exhaling a

plume of fag vapour.

'Can't sell you any tenderloin, haha.'

His boorishness made me even more excited about snatching away his livelihood.

'Could you come into the office?' I said, careful not to say please.

He shook his head and exhaled a dragonly jet. 'Knew it,' he said, half-laughing. 'I'm getting the boot, aren't it?'

I paused, trying to crystalise the moment in my memory. 'Yes,' I said. 'Your contract's being terminated. Gross misconduct.'

Instead of exploding he calmly sucked his electrofag. 'Paul ordered this didn't he?' he said. 'Fucking coward couldn't do it himself. Where is he? Fucking prick's going to hospital.'

He's in his office, I said, disbelieving of my good luck. I hoped Paul would be beaten to a paste and ideally lose the use of his legs.

Salman threw his mug at the wall and it smashed in rounded shards. He spat tea in my face but otherwise I was unharmed. It was Paul he wanted.

I deliberated watching the spectacle but couldn't risk having to step in. How would I decide which of them to assist? Best make a calming cup of tea, I thought.

I took a seat and listened. Paul was trying to reason with the beast, his reedy voice sneering about 'restructuring' as glass smashed and folders bounced off walls. Salman was roaring like an animal and I thought I heard a crack. Had he punched Paul in the face?

The commotion caught the attention of two warehousemen smoking in the delivery bay (Paul had tried banning fag breaks and almost had his car torched as a result) who scurried towards the office hoping for a glimpse of the violence. They peered in and took photographs, laughing hysterically as Paul gasped and pleaded. Was he being strangled?

Disappointingly the struggle then ceased. Silence. A

third voice, unfamiliar, spoke over the din. It was rhythmic and firm, an authoritative rumble that silenced them both. I edged to the door to see Salman being frogmarched out by Stephen Maltby, whose enormous hand was clamped onto the back of his neck. Salman barked in pain and his head shunted back and forth like a breeze block.

'Get off me you prick!' he said. His arm was twisted behind his back like a wishbone and I willed Maltby to break it. *Go on,* I thought. *Crush his bones to dust.*

Paul emerged with a cut on his head and ribbons of blood down his face. Salman hadn't killed him (more's the pity) but he'd left an admirable impact crater. Maltby barrelled through the warehouse and shoved Salman out through the delivery entrance, tossing him from the premises like an unsellable cabbage.

Paul ushered me into his office. He was trembling and his fingers shook as he peeled open a pot of milk jelly. He spooned it into his mouth and immediately opened another, then another, then another. Six pots later, and with jelly still quivering on his tongue, he took a breath.

'Wow, hehe hehe. I don't even, hehe, I don't know what was that about, hehe.'

He gibbered like a baby, pretending not to have expected such a reaction. 'He just came at me, hehe hehe.'

His chuckles no longer signaled lighthearted awkwardness, they were now aggressive, anxious tics disrupting his sentences and impairing his speech.

'Would you like more milk jelly?' I said, unfussed whether he lived or died.

'Hehe, that'd be nice, hehe hehe.' he said.

I peeled off a foil lid and thrust the pot in his face. I deliberated landing him a discretionary thump while he was still in shock but reconsidered in a fit of ignoble compassion. *If only I'd been born a psychopath,* I thought.

He'd wiped the blood from his face revealing the entirety of his wound. It was a plummy purple protrusion that bulged from his eye like a garden slug, beneath which

146

were dark clouds of bruising threaded with pink seams of blood. His eyeball was buried beneath the swelling while his good eye hung bloodshot and glazed.

'The customers can't see me like this,' he said. 'I need to get to hospital.'

He tipped the remaining milk jellies into his backpack and zipped on a sorrowful blue fleece. (Where did one buy such things?) 'Tell the team I'm at head office, make it sound important.'

He tumbled out of the service entrance and through the car park, shielding his face from the precious customers as he fussed with car keys and bloodied bog roll. His windscreen was sticky with phlegm – a parting gift from Salman – forcing him to wipe it with a sleeve cuff, leaving wet streaks across the glass. Further inspection revealed a cracked rear window, a dented bonnet and an arc of urine up the bumper.

Once he'd driven off I finished my tea and clocked off early, untroubled by diligence or tedious commitment to work.

I arrived home to see Jasper's car, a blubbery little hatchback emblazoned with the Gadswood logo, parked outside. Was he further reducing my square footage? Fearing a mucosal gumming fee I resisted spitting on it, half-heartedly booting the bumper. It brought little comfort. If only I knew how to make a car bomb, I thought, gleefully imagining his skull being blown to pieces.

Upstairs he was leaning in my doorway making notes in a leather docket. 'Hey bud,' he said, quickly closing the folder. 'You're home early. What's going on, dude?'

I mumbled something about work and pushed past him, viciously hungry. I'd eaten a muddy radish for lunch and my stomach was pulsating like a jellyfish bell.

'Still got a few payments outstanding on your account bud.' said Jasper. He passed me a bill quoting the total for which I was liable. It was more than I'd earn in six months.

Scanning down the page I noticed I'd been charged an unarranged subletting fee of two hundred pounds.

'What's that?' I said.

'Insurance costs for a second tenant bud,' he said. 'Totally standard practice.'

'But no one else lives here,' I said, careful not to appear uncooperative. 'Who's the second tenant?'

'Hate to disagree with you bud, but we heard on the grapevine that Sheena's been staying here. 'Two bodies, two tenants.'

I tried vainly to explain the situation with the prostitute but he was busy typing figures into his phone.

'Need to get a payment from you today if that's okay bud. Are you good for the full balance?'

He produced a card reader and looked at me expectantly.

'Can I pay you next month?' I said, convinced the debt would follow me to my grave.

'No can do, I'm afraid,' he said. 'Need to get it paid today. Can't risk it affecting our working capital.'

I wondered what the hell working capital meant. Was it something to do with invoices?

'Gonna need your card, bud.'

He held out his hand. His presumptuousness was incredible. Why did everyone think I was rich?

'I'm sorry, I can't pay you now.' I said.

His charm darkened into a glare and he took a step towards me. 'I'm not leaving here without a payment.' he said.

I edged away but the room was so small I bumped into the partition wall, causing it to bow like a wobble board. He rose like a haunched serpent, baring his teeth and eclipsing my vision with a stare that'd haunt me until my death.

'*Give me your debit card,*' he said, so close my cheeks were ruddied by his breath. '*Now.*'

My fingers were slippy and my hands trembled like a virgin boy's. I dug into my pockets to retrieve the card and thrust it at him, terrified of the monster before me.

'That's it,' he said. 'That wasn't so difficult was it?'
I was still shuddering. A veil of shock had enshrouded me and I wanted nothing except to cry.

His arms had slowly closed around me and he held me to his chest. I was cloaked by a sudden warmth; a rush of comfort not dissimilar to a nourishing stab of heroin. I sniffed as flicks of chest hair tickled my nostrils and caramel cologne lightly fingered my senses.

'You've done the right thing,' he said. 'Let me do the rest.'

He smoothed my hair and gently sat me on the bed. 'Here,' he said, passing me a flask. 'Have a sip of this. It'll calm you down.'
I recognised the sweet, soapy burn of Alcomax and gulped it down. The shock was subsiding but my cheeks still trembled.

'I've just got to make a call. Will you be alright, bud?'
He spoke so soothingly I felt a tear dribble down my face. He offered me a tissue and for a moment seemed like my only friend in the world.

'I'll be back, okay?'
I nodded and he left the room.

A soft tap caused the partition to flutter.

'Are you okay?' came Sheena's voice from the other side. She sounded sad and distant.

'I'm fine.' I said. The Alcomax enabling me to speak with renewed coherence.

'What's happening?' she said. 'Did he hit you?'
I reassured her Jasper was simply collecting a payment and that there was nothing for her to worry about.

'Are you sure?' she said, 'It sounded like banging.'
The discussion was cut mercifully short when Jasper re-entered the room with an eerie, unknowable smile.

'All sorted,' he said, handing back my debit card. 'You should be proud of yourself bud. Nobody likes debt hanging over them.'

I felt a rise of elation and almost smiled. 'Thank you.' I

said.

He clapped my shoulder and straightened his tie. 'Catch you soon, okay bud? Keep up the good work.'

I reassured him I would.

'Almost forgot,' he said, unzipping the docket. 'This month's fees.' He laid an envelope by the fishtank. 'Gonna need that asap, okay?'

Okay, I said.

When he'd gone I opened the bill and read down the charges. Besides the usual (agency liaison recreation allowance, quarterly structural maintenance stipend) they'd added a 'transaction and processing' fee of twenty-two pounds, debited upon receipt of my payment. Were they charging me to pay my own debts?

I was roused by another knock on the wall.

'Can I come over?' said Sheena. 'It's important.'

She sat on the bed staring at my newspaper patchwork.

'Would you like a tomato?' I said.

She shook her head and her mouth hung open, limp and slack. I'd not thought it possible to see her more miserable but here she sat, motionless and glum.

'Are you alright?' I said, dunking the tomato in the fishtank.

'I just wanted to say goodbye,' she said. Was she going to kill herself? 'Jasper's evicting me.'

I untensed, glad suicide was off the cards.

'And I'm going to kill myself.'

My mouth opened but I said nothing.

'I'm doing it tonight,' she said. 'Poison.'

She pulled a small polythene wrap from her pocket. Inside was a powdery grey substance like ground coriander. Did she have a mortal herb intolerance?

'What's that?' I said.

'Arsenic. I managed to get hold of the real thing. Undercooking the rice wasn't working.'

Despite suicide being the only logical escape, I worried for her. 'Where did you get it?' I said.

'From the coal pit. Apparently there's loads of it down there. Killed a lot of miners, this did.'

She explained how the pit manager had sourced the arsenic in exchange for a lunchtime back rub. 'He gets rhomboid pain.' she said.

I stared at the silvery compound. 'I don't think it's a good idea,' I said. 'What if it goes wrong?'

She raised an eyebrow, gently amused. 'How wrong could it go?'

I bit into the tomato.

CHAPTER 22

I awoke the next morning to an excited knock on the partition wall.

'Good news!' said Sheena. 'Can I come over?' *Was she speaking from heaven?*

I untangled my sleepy old testicles and clicked on the kettle. *I need to steal more teabags,* I thought, noting my dwindling supply.

Sheena tumbled through the door, uncharacteristically joyful. Shouldn't she be vomiting blood by now?

'Guess what?' she said.

I hoped she'd not been researching alternative methods of suicide (apparently drowning was euphoric).

'What?' I said, surprised to be holding my breath.

'I got a job.'

I exhaled loudly and saw her smile for the third time in my life.

'Oh wow!' I said. 'Where?'

'At your supermarket!'

I was perplexed. I'd heard nothing about this. 'When did that happen?' I said. 'When was your interview?'

'Didn't have one,' she said. 'Apparently they just liked the sound of me. They want me in straight away.'

I poured the tea and sat on the bed. Sheena bounced around the room like a squash ball, utterly thrilled at her new appointment.

'Peter Whamley phoned last night,' she said. 'I was *literally* about to take the arsenic. Said he wanted to register me, get my CV jazzed up, all that stuff. He's very thorough, isn't he? Went through everything. My background, my health, my family; he said I'm exactly what they're looking for.'

I was immediately dubious of such good fortune (Dad had once returned a lost cat and been rewarded with a punch in the mouth), assuming something fiendish was occurring behind the scenes. Might Whamley make her a staffroom concubine?

'Means I can give up muckraking,' she said. 'Thank fuck.'

'What about the coal pit?' I said. 'Will you still have to break rocks?'

'I'm gonna do the Sunday shift while I'm on probation, just in case, y'know. Keep my options open.'

That's a good idea, I said, convinced Paul would sack her once she'd served her purpose. What *was* her purpose, exactly? Her appointment directly contradicted the cost-saving strategy I'd been hired to expedite.

'Are you a contractor?' I said.

'Full-time,' she said. 'Permanent.'

Even more baffling. Had Whamley called in a favour on my behalf? Beside the administrative pitfalls there simply wasn't locker room for another full-timer. The contractors already struggled for coat space, fearful after Linda had warned she'd 'torch the fuck' out of any jacket found hanging near her designated peg.

'I start on Monday.' she said, sipping her tea and smiling again.

∞

I'd been required to arrive at work humiliatingly early because Paul wanted to take me on a store 'walkaround' (supposedly a contractual obligation) during which he'd teach me about merchandising and shelf end displays.

His wound had been stitched closed but his eye was still buried beneath the pulpy blue swelling. Salman must've really walloped him (and rightly so).

'How's your eye?' I said, hoping it'd been infected and required painful extraction.

'Oh I'll live, hehe.' he said, confirming the exact opposite of what I wished.

The store was bright and silent and he led me through the aisles, occasionally straightening a protruding cereal box.

'Do you know much about retail merchandising?' he said.

'No.' I said, barely even listening.

'It's a dark art, hehe,' he said, implying some kind of witchcraft was at play. 'It's all about drawing the customer in.'

We stopped and he pointed to the priciest cat food, a weighty sack of jelly biscuits. 'Notice anything about this?' he said, thrilled to be imparting such worthless knowledge.

'No.' I said. *I hate you, idiot.* I'd been made to wake an hour early for this, time I could've spent slicing turnips or demoulding the bedclothes.

He flicked his finger between the shelf and his face. 'See it now?'

'No.' I said. Was it something to do with shelf strips?

'Eye level,' he said. 'Put the premium items at eye level to draw the customer in. Clever, eh? Hehe.'

'Won't they just look up or down?' I said, deliberately facetious. I was tired and quarrelsome after drinking a celebratory bottle of mouthwash with Sheena last night.

'They can, but statistics tell us more products are sold when placed at eye level.'

That's interesting. I said, hoping he'd be crushed in a pallet truck accident.

He advised on the intricacies of gantry presentation and clip strips, gondola shelving and pegboard panelling, stopping only to glug from a water bottle he'd filled with double cream.

'I'm thinking of rolling this out to the shopfloor staff, what do you think?'

I knew the staff, and Linda in particular, would detest such a lecture. 'That's a great idea,' I said. 'I think it'd really help them.'

He smiled and his overbite jutted out like a cliff edge. 'Do you think so? Wow, that's great, thanks, hehe.'

It was then I glimpsed his insecure and desperate side, a man who'd sleep sounder knowing such useless initiatives had been implemented. How unfathomable to derive such satisfaction from one's job, I thought, still labouring under the assertion that the working world was little more than a festering, cavernous sump.

'I'll draw up a training schedule, hehe.' he said.

Back in the office he peeled open a rice pudding and handed me a folder. I opened it and saw Sheena's name.

'We've got a new starter,' he said. 'She'll be a great addition to the team.'

I said nothing. I didn't want to jeopardise her fortuity by asking impertinent questions but her appointment left me uneasy.

'What's she like?' I said. 'Did you interview her?'

'Didn't need to,' he said. 'She's perfect.'

'Has she got any experience?' I said, fully aware she had nothing of the sort.

'Let's just say she ticks a lot of boxes, hehe.' he said, winking as if we were friends.

'Like what?'

His eyes bulged in mock frustration, irritated at my inability to decipher his code.

'Have a look at her application, that should answer a few questions.'

Why don't you just tell me, idiot?

We were interrupted by a knock at the door and I turned to see Stephen Maltby standing at the glass, ominously tensing his jaw. Was he chanting? He closed his eyes when Paul ushered him in. 'I'm here now.' he said, slowly uncurling his tongue.

Returning to my office I leafed through Sheena's folder

and noticed how particular details had been struck through with pink highlighter *(one lung, suicidal thoughts, dead father, benefit claimant)* and were annotated with effusive markings: 'yes!', 'perfect' and, most mysteriously: 'better than S'.

It all then became clear: Sheena was Paul's charity project. Her single lung qualified her as disabled while her godawful home life was the very picture of urban destitution. Her parents' denouement compounded her status as a piteous martyr and her suicidal tendencies clearly required extensive therapy. Paul was right – she *was* perfect. She met (and exceeded) every requirement necessary for him to fulfil his rehabilitation quota and get his name in the store magazine. The HR director would be left reeling, wondering why Salman was ever a concern.

I completed the necessary paperwork, printed Sheena's name badge and set aside a uniform. I was immeasurably relieved she'd no longer be required to fry bacon for her board directors but concerned her misfortune was being preyed upon. My concern was quickly subsumed by jealousy when I noticed her salary exceeded mine. Must I stab myself in the lung for a payrise?

∞

As the weeks passed I became gloriously skilled in the dismissal process. My earlier prattle, so unwieldy and cumbersome on Dean, had been streamlined into a sweeping dictatorial flourish delivered with unabashed heartlessness. Having eviscerated nearly half of the original workforce, my job was made easier still when the remaining few began seeking employment elsewhere, an endeavour I magnanimously granted them time off to pursue. ('Of *course* you can leave early for a job interview.' I'd say, knowing full well Paul would deduct the hours from their redundancy settlements.)

This left only Linda. Her submissive goblins, so forceful as a united offering, had been systematically picked off and replaced by timid, docile contractors, all of whom were firmly under Paul's command. She seemed smaller now, a diminutive figure among the towering groceries over which she once presided.

This afternoon she sat alone in the staffroom, leafing through magazines with a sad resolve on her face.

'Alright Porkchop?' she said with a resigned smile. Her tone had thawed, like a hospice patient seeking atonement before returning to the earth.

'I'm okay.' I said. Should I ask how she was? Obviously I didn't care a jot but it seemed the civilised thing to do. 'Are you alright?'

She looked at me and we exchanged a moment of warmth.

'Yeah I suppose so,' she said. 'Just waiting for the boot now. Looking for new jobs, all that shit.'

She wasn't stupid – she knew redundancy was looming. I gathered she was counting on a severance package based on the nine years she'd spent with the company, money that'd sustain her during the oncoming spell of joblessness. She'd not, however, counted on Paul's obsessive, almost psychotic desire to cut costs and report better numbers. Returning to the office I found him fidgeting with Linda's contract and muttering to himself.

'Oh, hiya, hehe,' he said, spineless idiot. 'I've been looking at this redundancy payout for Linda.'

Why don't you put a gun in your mouth? I thought.

'Seems like she's due a pretty penny, hehe.'

The total figure was a little below three thousand pounds, barely enough to cover Aunt Tasmin's quarterly Thrushman's budget.

'Any way we can get that down a bit?' He squinted at me from his jellied, bulbous eye. 'Ideally down to zero, hehe.'

I said nothing. Redundancy pay was a legal right, surely?

His teeth jutted out like a gopher. 'Have we got any dirt on her? Anything that'd count as gross misconduct?'

'No,' I said, eliciting a hideous grimace.

'In that case we might need to find something. Can I leave it with you? Anything – poo, stealing, whatever. It's just I've got that money earmarked for something else. Can't go wasting it on a lost cause, hehe.'

'What if I can't find anything?' I said, perfectly reasonably.

'Unfortunately that type of thing gets considered at your probationary hearing. If you can't get the job done that's a red flag I'm afraid.'

He said this as though it were an officiated process and not a discretionary decision made by him alone.

'Fine,' I said. 'I'll find something.'

Despite her utter fatuousness Linda was a skilled and slippery quarry, able to goad and sneer without ever causing a sackable level of offence. Her skill lay in the fear she instilled in others, a snarling disregard for their sensitivities, possessions and beliefs that left them crushed and beaten in her path. She'd alienated the contractors to the point where they'd hover fretfully outside the staffroom if she were inside, nervously waiting for her break to finish before venturing to the kettle.

'I ain't havin' some tosser nicking my teabags.' she said, her words falling flat now Salman wasn't around to laugh at her fervent stupidity.

She became increasingly isolated, often conducting phone calls with ex-staffers during which she'd complain loudly about the store's inglorious decline.

'It's like a fuckin' museum,' she cawed. 'All the old lot's gone, it's just me and a bunch of part-timers now.'

Her tone, brash and hateful as always, betrayed a longing for something lost: systems she'd once relied upon that'd now been dismantled and airlifted from her life like superfluous pylons. For Linda it wasn't simply a job, it was *everything*. I'd read about people like her in lifestyle magazines. Party planners, brewers, designers – people for whom a job wasn't merely a humiliating scrum in a cold swamp but an enriching vocational pleasure from which

159

they gleaned genuine satisfaction.

I monitored her in an attempt to record some misstep or wrongdoing but she was as wily as she was boorish, evidently unwilling to repeat Dean's and Salman's mistakes.

There was, however, one avenue down which I'd not ventured, a confidence I could break in the absence of anything sufficiently incriminating – that of the stolen goods stockpiled throughout her house. It'd be my word against hers, of course, but there was no doubt onto whose side Paul would come down. He'd mentioned that sacking Linda would be like 'taking down a warhorse' and that I was to utilise all available resources to complete the task, up to and including fabricated abuse claims and corporate smear tactics.

'Some prisoners last for weeks without breaking.' he'd added cryptically, leaving me questioning whether he had soldiers' blood on his hands. Had he tortured military captives?

My caution arose from the violence with which she'd threatened me should I ever divulge the details of our unconsummated tryst; cautionary advice made all the more frightening after my encounter with her cousin. Despite my intoxication the evening had clung to me, her spitting excrement noises permeating my thoughts at the idlest of moments, haunting my dreams in the form of rainstorms and untethered hosepipes.

Besides the stolen store supplies it seemed there was little else I could use against her. Consulting the contractors had proved a fallow exercise, for none dared speak out for fear of broken bones.

'I heard her cousin broke an old woman's legs,' said one terrified colleague. 'I don't want that happening to my grandma.'

I tried to empathise but had no frame of reference. *My grandma was a callous old gargoyle who'd rigged inhumane bird traps and tortured them once caught. As a* child I was made to sweep bloodied feathers from the patio and pick wing bones from the scrabbled mesh of the rats' cage.

'She's harmless,' said Mum, failing to fool even herself. Unfortunately Linda's insults and threats were meaningless if uncorroborated, leaving me to face either a beating or a potential sacking. It was Sheena who ultimately made up my mind, reminding me that two broken legs would net me both a nourishing stretch in hospital and several weeks off work.

'Tell her I did it,' she said, her eyes twinkling with promise. 'I'd happily take a thumping if it meant free food and a warm place to sleep.'

And thus I made the decision to turn her in. I drafted the paperwork and sat as Paul read it through.

'This is good,' he said. 'Really good, hehe.' He continued down the page and narrowed his eyes. 'Any way we can er, *embellish* it a little?'

What do you mean, tosser? I thought. His hair was cropped shorter today and I wondered what kind of criminal might charge money for such a service.

'I cut it myself, you know,' he said, clocking my interest. 'You should see what some of these hairdressers charge, it's crazy. You know me though, always keen to make a saving, hehe.'

Returning to the document he asked: 'can we bump this up a bit? It'd be good to throw the book at her, you know, make doubly sure she doesn't get her hands on that redundancy money. I've got it earmarked for something else, you see.'

'Yes, I know.' I said. What might he need the money for so urgently?

'Maybe change this bit.' He drew my attention to the section where I'd listed the stolen goods I'd seen in Linda's house. 'Instead of putting just *bleach, tampons and toilet roll*, could we add in some premium items? Maybe a computer or a case of champagne?'

I explained that this would be an obvious lie but he didn't seem fussed. 'Stealing's stealing,' he said. 'We just need to massage the facts a little bit.'

'Fine,' I said, tired of his dithering cruelty. 'Put whatever you like.'

His eyes danced in their sockets, buoyant behind the glasses. 'Great,' he said. 'Always better to go in strong, hehe.'

The documentation was signed and I was required to schedule a meeting with Linda to dole out the sacking. The prospect stirred in me an unquantifiable guilt, a groundswell of concern that found me questioning my previously unswerving hatred. Perhaps I simply hated my*self* for bending to Paul's autocratic whims; for ruining peoples' lives as a cost-saving initiative for a corporation whose yearly turnover could comfortably afford them three hundred nuclear cruise missiles.

Nevertheless, if I were to pass my probation it was understood I'd need to plumb such depths. It was also important to remember that Linda had shown me nothing but the basest contempt, her sozzled pub flirtation presumably little more than an attempt to leverage me into her servitude. In addition, she'd gifted me a derogatory nickname and threatened to have me hospitalised. I had to remain firm.

Paul advised I schedule the meeting for a Friday afternoon, that way she could leave early and use the weekend to process the information. Despite such cynical reasoning I could only agree, the thought of her slatternly ire causing me an involuntary shiver. I wondered how Paul's car might fare once I'd broken the news. Would she rig it with explosives? *Don't dare to dream.*

On the morning of the sacking Paul called a staff meeting in the warehouse (he referred to these flockings as 'huddles', as if we were vagrants clustered around a burning skip). The cacophonous nattering of months' prior was gone, replaced by a gloomy hush as the contractors awaited his appearance, a king before the box baler. No longer did he require Linda's command over the gaggle of pigs, for the old guard were now all but purged, a misty memory in the minds of those who cared whether they lived or died (I didn't).

Paul clapped his hands and welcomed utter silence. His mouth coiled into a dorkish smile as he surveyed his dungeon of rats, cloying underlings over whom he held absolute power, a dominion of ants birthed right from his ejaculatory duct.

His eyes tumbled excitedly in his head. 'Hi, hi, thank you, thank you,' he said, gesticulating with ringmasterly flourishes. 'Great to see you all, hehe.' A pause. He leaned his jowly head forward expectantly. What did he *want* from us?

Long, tortuous seconds passed. I scanned the room. The contractors were silent, nonplussed, mystified. It was then, nestled in the grey, draughty stockroom surrounded by pallets of potted meat, that I beheld the single most heartbreaking and pitiful spectacle I'd ever witnessed. One of the throng, a thick, clammy little cashier named Seamus, began to clap. A solitary, repetitive thwack, he stared right at Paul as he did it, his eyes meek and pleading as his weathered hands beat together like haggis casings. I was hopelessly saddened but Paul's smile suggested this was, for him, a dream come true. Seamus was joined in his applause by Tracy, another contractor governed solely by fear, who was then joined by Abdus, then Warren, then József, before the entire workforce were clapping. Some were frantic, others embarrassed, but they all did it. All except Linda, whose hands remained clasped behind her back, and me, who'd rather ingest bin water than show respect of any kind to such a piteous wretch.

'Thank you, thank you,' said Paul, his conductorly hands quieting the din. 'Great you could all make it, hehe, hehe.' He glugged from a bottle of milk squash and wiped his lips. His manner suggested he'd now ascended to the throne of the gods. 'Just a few announcements, hehe.' He pinched his nose and took a breath. 'First things first. Unfortunately – and I hate to be the bearer of bad news – we'll soon be losing our *longest-serving member of staff*.'

A hush befell us. We all knew whom he meant but stared straight ahead, terrified of petrification by Linda's medusa stare. I was astonished. She'd not even been told of the sacking and yet here stood Paul, mouth white with dairy, announcing it publicly. Such callous indignity caused me a wobble, a stupefaction exacerbated by the ruby flush darkening Linda's cheeks. She said nothing. Her eely lips pursed and scissored and I thought her head might pop.

'Obviously she's been a great help to us over the years,' he continued, deeply condescending. 'But all good things must come to an end, hehe.'

The silence was overwhelming. Paul then extended his hand in her direction. 'Let's give her a round of applause shall we?'

The assembly resumed their applause, now solemn and stunted in contrast to the effusiveness they'd previously shown Paul. I suspected had he been receiving a handjob right then he couldn't have looked more pleased with himself.

'But we must push on,' he said. 'Onwards and upwards.'

Linda remained thunderously stern. She stared at Paul like he'd just desecrated Aunt Tasmin's grave, and despite her silence I'd never been more terrified of her.

He continued briskly, fussing with his glasses as he talked us through the retail merchandising training, calmly ignoring the hatred cast his way.

'We were going to get an external facilitator in,' he said, a note of feigned exhaustion in his voice. 'But head office have cut our budget *again*, meaning we'll need to, er, make a few savings here and there, hehe.'

This was obvious nonsense: the training was a bureaucratic ego trip he'd conjured out of nowhere, a means by which

164

to solidify his position as master and commander.

'I'll be running the first session on Friday morning,' he said. 'It's open to everyone so I look forward to seeing you all there, hehe.' He lay a clipboard on the baler. Attached by a string was a pen. 'Put your name down if you'd like to attend, it's important we know how many of you will be there, fire regulations and all that, hehe. Wouldn't want you to burn to death, hehe.' (In truth I imagined he would've *relished* the sight of a burning minion, if only to imbue his urine with an ounce of power.)

The huddle slowed to a close and there was a laboured groundswell of interest in the clipboard as everyone clamoured to be a team player. Something about it made me want to cry.

Linda disappeared and I noticed Paul watching her go, his lower jaw flagellating excitedly. His minions swarmed about him like honeyed flies and I scurried back to my office, sick and disgusted. To my surprise, Linda was already inside, sitting quietly at one of the desks.

'Oh hi,' I said. 'Are you alright?' She looked at me and her eyelid drooped. Had she been drinking Alcomax?

She clutched a coffee cup. 'Knew it was happening,' she said. 'Didn't think he'd do it like that though. Fuckin' tosser.'

I know, I said. *What a cretin.*

'Don't worry though,' she said. 'I'm seeing my cousin tonight. He'll fuckin' kill him.'

I hoped she meant *literally* kill him, for I'd certainly be first in the queue to urinate on the coffin should he pass: arcs of warm, amber piss raining into the grave trench (perhaps a dousing for his mother?) before Linda took her turn, squatting, using the headstone for balance, and unfunneling a diarrhetic blast into the earthy ditch. Salman, providing he wasn't in prison by then, surely wouldn't miss such an event, calmly waiting by the graveside for the chance to excrete a hot load over the sodden casket.

'Will he *really* kill him?' I said.

'Couldn't say for sure. He'll definitely break his neck.'

Was that a mortal injury? I dearly hoped so. She lit a Thrushman's, admirably flouting the smoking laws. 'Them rules are for cowards.' she said, reasonably enough. She exhaled towards the smoke detector. 'Right then, Porkchop, let's get this over with. Do what you need to do. Gimme my money and I'll fack off.' She coughed. 'Had enough of this shithole anyway.'

Not wishing to incriminate myself I said she'd been caught stealing by the CCTV cameras. This, of course, was a lie. Paul had long ago deactivated the cameras in an effort to reduce the store's energy expenditure, an initiative that won him a place at the company's Energy Awareness buffet. ('Better than my wedding day.' he'd said afterwards.)

She exhaled a cloud of brown smoke. 'What does that mean?' she said, very quietly. 'In terms of redundancy pay?'

I felt almost genuine remorse as the words left my mouth: 'It means you'll not get any.'

She stubbed out her Thrushman's on the desk and the anger swelled visibly inside her. She fingered her cigarette packet (it was sleeved in a protective casing on which was printed a St. George's cross) and breathed very slowly. Seconds passed, then minutes. *Agony.* Finally she spoke, almost at a whisper. 'What did you say?'

I clarified the decision regarding her lack of severance pay, reiterating how the decision had been Paul's alone and was nothing to do with me. 'It's out of my hands.' I said, lying like a champion.

Her fingers tightened around the coffee mug and I assumed, like Salman, that she'd hurl it at the wall.

'None at all?' she said, terrifyingly icy.

'No,' I said. 'As it's gross misconduct.'

Her fingers throbbed, puce, around the mug handle and I thought she'd crush it to dust with her bare hands. 'Okay then,' she said, easing off her grip. (Presumably she knew Paul would use such property damage to strengthen the case against her). 'That's me done then, is it? Nine years of work, down the fuckin' toilet.'

Despite my assertion that those nine years had been an utter, utter waste of time, I was, somewhat generously, on the cusp of apologising. This was quickly forgotten when she rose from the chair and addressed me directly. 'Thanks for *nothing*, Porkchop.' she said, sneering and nasty.

Her bilious tone reminded me what a slattern-mouthed idiot she really was: a feckless harridan on whom pity and compassion were hopelessly wasted. Thank *heavens* I'd not apologised, I thought, daydreaming about property foreclosures and kerbside penny begging.

She slammed the door on her way out and her footsteps receded down the corridor, stopping at Paul's office. I was genuinely excited. If Salman's pasting had been a marker of any kind, Linda would surely tear the eyeballs right out of his skull. My reverie was stalled by a stern, authoritative mumble, indiscernible to my ears, that quickly silenced her cawing. The voice was disappointingly familiar. Booming and resonant, her guttural squeals were all but bulldozed in its path.

Her footsteps were now disconsolate and slow, gradually falling away, lost amidst the revving baler and slobbering warehousemen. What on earth had happened? I cracked the door open and peeked around, quickly discerning the source of the exchange. Outside Paul's office was stationed Stephen Maltby, arms crossed and sleeves torn from his fleece like a military commando. Was he Paul's *bodyguard?*

Paul's spongy, oblong head then appeared from inside, peering after Linda.

'Coast clear?' he said.

A pause. 'I've made it so.' said Maltby, quizzically flaring his nostrils.

'Great stuff, hehe.' Paul's eyes darted towards me. 'Come inside, would you?' he said. 'Need to have a quick chat, hehe.'

I was astonished. Linda was supposed to have been our prize kill: a juggernaut whose sacking would require endless board meetings, HR consultations, legal quarrels and solicitors' input to eventuate, yet she'd walked out without so much as a globule of phlegm in Paul's direction. Had she some greater plan?

I sat opposite him and accidentally kicked over a case of milk water sitting beneath his desk.

Paul frowned. 'If you could, er, pick those up, that'd be great, hehe.'

I stared at him, repulsed. *Why don't you just kill yourself?* I thought.

It was then I felt a hand on my shoulder. Stephen Maltby was standing behind my chair, towering like a thunderous tree. 'You must do this.' he said, gouging his thumb into my trapezius. I winced in pain and lurched towards the floor, scrambling to pick up the bottles.

'Thank you, thank you,' said Paul. 'I like to run a tight ship, hehe.'

He seemed oddly confident and more repugnant than ever. 'Just wanted to follow up on the huddle.' he said. Stephen Maltby's breath heaved over me like a ship's piston.

'Head office have made more cuts so we're going to need to pick up some of the slack, hehe.'

I nodded petulantly. What might he make me do now? Kill someone? I'd happily knife him in the face if I knew I could get away with it. I imagined the courts being lenient in such a case, waiving my sentence and throwing a banquet in my honour.

Paul continued: 'Going to need you out on the shop floor if that's okay. We're all going to need to pitch in if we're going to meet this months' targets, hehe.'

'What do you mean 'on the shop floor'?' I said. 'Doing what?'

He shook his jowls and pressed his eyes closed, trying to elicit sympathy. 'Whatever needs doing.' he said. Then for good measure: 'your probation hearing's next week. I hope you've remembered.'

Stephen Maltby made a chant-like, droning sound.

'Yes.' I said, not mentioning that I'd thought of little else for the past three months. *A lifetime of interminable grunt labour*, I thought, profoundly saddened. *That's what I'm hoping for.*

CHAPTER 23

The week prior to my probationary hearing was arguably the worst of my life. It was the coldest winter for forty years, with freezing sleet bucketing in from morning till night, and winds so cold they froze the teeth in my skull. Negotiations between the bus drivers and their overlords had crumbled, leaving the services more disrupted than ever (the operator had vetoed the drivers' whisky allowance), meaning that most nights I faced a perishing two-hour journey home.

My shopfloor duties were *excruciating*. My hands had been torn to shreds by cardboard and my spine was buckled from the shopping bags I was forced to carry to customers' cars. For the most part, however, I was on greeting duty: loitering at the entrance and smiling at customers as I tried fruitlessly to disguise my nauseating contempt. Given it was a busy store the doors were open most of the day, ushering in sub-zero blasts which numbed my fingers and caused frostbite to gnaw at my face.

I saw little of Paul. He remained ensconced in his office with Stephen Maltby standing guard, guzzling rice cream and refusing visitors of any kind. Only a handful of times did I see him on the shopfloor, fussing with shelf strips and berating co-workers for askew name badges or untucked work shirts. More often than not he'd send them home and advise they come back tomorrow having adjusted their attitude, attributing such tardiness to a chronic lack of respect. The victims never argued, for any whiff of dissent was quickly curbed by an ominous growl from Maltby, ever present at Paul's elbow, suggesting they fall into line. It proved an effective display of power, reinforcing Paul's authority while saving him half a day's wages.

In addition to the lavatories and staffroom floors, staff were now required, every two days, to wash Paul's car. He'd laminated a bulleted list of guidelines for how it was to be done ('mud dislodged from tyre treads', 'exhaust pipe waxed', etc.) and rigorously inspected the vehicle after each scrubbing. Were he unsatisfied with the result, the contractor was required to start anew, usually missing the last bus and, on more than one occasion, collapsing from cold shock.

My probationary hearing was scheduled for Tuesday, also Sheena's first day on the payroll. I'd tried scheduling in a meeting with Paul to discuss the agenda but his door remained closed, a strip of black adhesive covering the glass so I couldn't see inside. I tried appealing to Stephen Maltby but he simply rocked back and forth, singing at an almost inaudible level.

'Can I go in for five minutes?' I said. 'I need to speak to him about my meeting.'

Maltby didn't move. I thought I saw his pectorals twitch.

'Please let me in,' I said. 'It's important.'

Silence. He stood like a lump of iron, monolithic and cold. 'It's not your time.' he said serenely, staring into the distance, seemingly not of this world. (Was he looking at compost bags?)

I stamped back to work in a fury. Ordinarily I'd let off steam by spitting on Paul's car but it was being washed by a contractor and guarded by another, their faces blue with cold as the sleet lashed their attenuated frames.

This is worse than a Siberian labour camp, I thought, reasoning that at least labour camp inmates didn't live in fear of the sack. I retired to the staffroom and, in the absence of tea, poured a drink of water. Hot drinks were a thing of the past (Paul had sold the kettle on a bric-a-brac website) while the microwave had been moved into his office in a 'privilege redistribution' initiative. This left a cold tap, a fridge reeking of spoilt cream and a cupboard littered with vile, yellowing crockery.

The little table, once Linda and Salman's mithering forum (incredibly, I missed those days), now sat empty, ignored but for the printed instruction memo left by Paul every morning. This listed each employee and specified their daily duties, their allocated lunchbreak (a twenty-minute slot decided by Paul) and their cleaning assignments. (Those required to wash his car were highlighted a bright orange.)

I sipped the freezing, diaphanous water and raged at Paul's fatuousness. I'd previously assumed, given the unpleasantness of my role and the duties therein, that a successful probationary hearing was a certainty, yet I couldn't help but feel a snap of doubt as I swallowed the limescale flakes that danced in my glass.

I'd resolved to contact Peter Whamley, reasoning he might provide some sound advice regarding my meeting with Paul. Foregoing the stillness of a Saturday, I'd ridden the bus to Crumbford and watched a pensioner get mauled by a hooligan's dog, an ordeal the owner chalked up to 'dodgy tripe mix.'

His office was, somewhat expectedly, a heartbreaking shambles, worse even than during my last visit. Lager cans spilled from the bin and in a far corner lay a mattress, yellow and stained, suggesting he now slept here. In place of a duvet was a patchwork of folders, stapled together like an administrative quilt. The relentless cold snap had left bruises of mould around the windows and the walls saturated; peeling paintwork turning green as the outer walls sprouted patches like clustered liverspots.

He too was green: a thin, sallow ghoul from whom life had drained like a de-roofed ovarian cyst. His shirt hung baggy and limp around his once-voluminous gut and the skin beneath his neck fell, grey and loose, about his collar.

'It's you,' he said, easing the door open. 'Y'brought any beer?'

I explained how every penny I earned went directly to Gadswood's, an arrangement I foresaw continuing until I was happily dead and buried.

He exhaled tiredly and his chest heaved with asthma. 'Fookin' mould.' he said, struggling for breath. I sympathised, achingly familiar with Gadswood's policy of ignoring damp problems until the tenant was hospitalised or simply perished. ('I'm not your mum, dude,' Jasper had said, leaning over my sick bed with a chip and pin machine. 'Can't drop everything 'cos you've got a sniffle.')

The office was dark and glacially cold. There were icicles dribbling from the windowsill and the walls ran wet with frost. Whamley pulled a tarpaulin around his shoulders and hobbled to the sink. 'Fancy a brew?'

'Yes please.' I said.

At least you can still enjoy a brew, I thought. *Maybe all's not lost.*

From beneath the sink he fetched out a mess tin that'd been collecting the runoff from a rusty pipe. The water was brown and freezing and I wondered if he might soon die of cholera.

'It's not the fookin' Ritz,' he said, clocking my concern. 'But it works, alright?'

Holding the tin aloft he wafted the underside with the flame of cigarette lighter, wheezing as his arms fell tired.

'Shall I help?' I said.

'Aye, hold this tin for me,' he said. 'I need to get right underneath it.'

I complied, my fingers pincing as he held the lighter in place.

'Won't be much longer,' he said. 'Usually takes about an hour.'

'What happened to the kettle?' I said. *Had Gadswood's repossessed it?*

'Fookin' thing froze up,' he said. 'Left it in a crossbreeze.'

Having boiled the water, he filled two half-scissored lager cans and plucked some teabags from a dish.

'What's that?' I said, noting a spray can by the sink.

'Fixative,' he said. 'Spray that on a fookin' teabag and it'll last you three days.'

I stared at his emaciated face. His chalky skin and protruding bones suggested he'd been gutted, quite exhaustively, by Gadswood's. Given his were business premises I assumed he was liable for the commercial licensing *and* private enterprise fees, both prohibitively expensive tariffs that increased the rent to that of a small castle.

'What's on your mind?' he said, easing into a swivel chair.

'I've got a probationary hearing this week,' I said. 'I need some advice. Paul won't talk to me.'

Whamley craned his shoulder, implying a sprain of some kind. (Had Jasper been beating him?) 'Do you like the job?' he said, quite unexpectedly.

Involuntarily I laughed. 'Of course not,' I said. 'Nobody *likes* their job, do they?'

Begging to differ, he relayed his experiences with luthiers and fashion buyers, people who loved their jobs because they were roles for which they'd diligently studied and not pits of hopelessness they'd arrived at through laziness and bad luck.

'If you don't like it, fookin' write it off,' he said, thumbing his clavicle. 'Find something else.'

'*What?*' I said, marginally flummoxed. Given my hellish two-hour bus ride I'd at least expected some semblance of a strategy. 'But what about my meeting?' I said. 'Haven't you got any advice?'

'That *is* my fookin' advice,' he said, scratching a lesion on his neck. 'He's obviously not keeping you on. You've served your purpose, now you're out on your fookin' ear.'

I blinked momentarily. 'Surely he wouldn't.' I said, knowing it was *exactly* the kind of thing Paul might do. (He'd once boasted of sacking a woman whose fingernails were 'too much'.)

'Think what y'like,' he said, folding the tarpaulin over his knees. 'It's 'appenin.'

∞

Heartbreakingly, Whamley was right.

That Tuesday I arrived early for work, subconsciously trying to make a good impression (as if the decision hadn't been made months ago) by fussing with folders and hoping the sifting of papers would alert Paul to my presence.

Why do I even care? I thought, a needle of pride dragging at my side. I could hear Stephen Maltby's thick, resonant breath from the corridor and hoped, in some naive way, that I might have stockpiled enough goodwill to warrant a successful outcome. The meeting was scheduled for five-thirty, a strategy Paul used to ensure any backlash was kept to a minimum and didn't impact the working day. Having been the executioner so many times myself, it was maddening to be strung along in such a way, and even worse knowing it'd probably been planned all along.

The hour arrived and Stephen Maltby collared me on the shopfloor where I was bruising fruit in an effort to make it unsellable. It was something I did whenever I had the chance, later scavenging the tainted items from the wheelie bin and pickling them for longevity.

'The time has come, the soldier said,' said Maltby, his words predictably perplexing. 'To talk of apron strings.'

I tossed back a courgette and strode after him. *There goes dinner*, I thought, hungry and defeated. As usual, the store was busy for this time of day. Pallid office workers shuffled the aisles like reanimated corpses, their stooped frames and downcast features suggestive of a working life unenviable to even the most downtrodden of sweatshop minions. *It could be worse*, I thought, watching them paw at harissa and tussle over the diminished blueberry stock.

Maltby walked in silence but sporadically swung his arms around in flailing, rotative motions. Was he dancing? We arrived at Paul's office and he tapped out a strange, rhythmic knocking on the door. 'What is language?' he said, scintillating in his peculiarity. Before I even understood the question Paul had called us in, his reedy voice infuriating even when muffled through a wall.

His office was darker than I remembered. It smelt like a faulty refrigerator, ripe with butter and binbag sweat. His desk, previously so ordered and meticulous, stood cluttered with yoghurt lids, cheese rinds, milk bottles. I went to sit down but Maltby caught my arm and held me back, his grip like a hose clamp. Seated behind his computer, Paul gave a slight nod, a signal that I was to be unhanded, and I thumped into a seat, thoroughly disquieted.

'Probationary meeting,' said Paul, devoid of his characteristic snigger. 'Not good news I'm afraid.'

'What do you mean?' I said.

'You've not passed. Sorry.'

He clearly felt not one shred of contrition, distracted by a blob of custard.

'What?' I said, flapping and crazed. 'What the *fuck?*'

'Just procedure I'm afraid,' he said, wildly unfazed at the desecration of my livelihood. He nodded at Maltby. 'Stephen will sort out the details, paperwork and so on. Let him know if you've got any problems. Now, if you don't mind, I've really got to get on. Lots to get through this week.' He scooped up the custard and sucked it off his finger. 'Thanks again.' he said.

'I don't understand,' I said. 'What's happening? What have I done?'

He turned back to his computer and squinted through his glasses. I stood, statuesque, staring. Should I scream at him? Slap him in the mouth? (I'd later regret such indecision, wishing I'd at least had the fortitude to spit in his face or pour milk down his back.) Instead I was collared by Maltby, frogmarched from the room and deposited in the corridor. Behind me the lock twisted in the door, solidifying my ruination. Without a job I'd be back on the dole, a terrifying prospect given the 'benefits and entitlements' appendix in my tenancy agreement, a clause that obligated me not only to gift them every penny of my benefits, but also to forfeit the remainder of my tenants' rights. This included running water, a gas supply, even lockable doors. 'We'd need to get inside dude, make sure you've not killed yourself,' said Jasper, maddeningly convincing. 'That's what people do when they're on the dole.'

I stumbled through the store as if through gauze, slamming into shoppers like they were carcasses in the meat basement. I reached the entrance and aimed, almost robotically, for Paul's car. In lieu of a petrol bomb I planned to urinate on it, perhaps even slash a tyre, but was halted by the two contractors on washing duty.

'Can't let you near the car,' said one, an exhausted little grub whose lips had frozen blue. 'More than my job's worth.'

I tried explaining how Paul would sack them at a moment's notice should he source cheaper labour. 'You've got no rights at all,' I said. 'He's got no loyalty. He just sacked *me!*'

The second contractor, József, a malnourished Hungarian, smiled imperceptibly, a victorious snark that said *you're just like the rest of us.* Did he welcome my downfall?

Propelled by a monstrous fury, I flew at them, unbuttoning my trousers and gobbing phlegm into the sluicing black sky. They blocked my path, hauling me from the car with unprecedented drone strength.

'Get back!' said the blue-lipped one. 'I ain't losing my

job 'cause of you, prick.'

József was silent, his arm locked tightly around mine as he yanked me backwards. With sleet lashing my face I tried vainly to warn them of Paul's mania. 'He'll replace you with child labour!' I cried, knowing full well this wasn't something he'd ruled out. (He'd once floated the idea of onboarding a classroom of twelve year-olds to cover the Christmas rush, an initiative he'd justified as a 'community work experience provision').

'Just keep away from the car.' they said.

If only I'd been able to sack you, I thought, throbbing with hatred and disgust. I spat on the ground near the car (scant consolation for the indignity I'd suffered) and scrambled to the bus stop. Ongoing industrial action meant the bus didn't arrive for an hour and a half, a perishing ordeal after which my desire to be killed in a traffic accident had subsided.

CHAPTER 24

I arrived home to find the door open and chatter from inside. Was I being burglarised? I eased it open, steeling myself for a confrontation with a thug or football supporter. I was so tired and angry that should such an altercation occur I'd simply crumple into a fitful heap, nipping at the intruder like a frightened squirrel.

Disappointingly I found Jasper inside, sprawled on the bed with a Thrushman's in his mouth and a phone clasped to his ear. He held a bottle of cava and took intermittent glugs as he spoke. 'I've gotta go dude,' he said, pretending I was more important than his phone call. 'Call me when they're out, okay? Any problems, tell them we'll take their kids away.' A pause. 'Haha, yeah, nice one, thanks again dude.' He hung up. 'Just a bit of business,' he said. 'Evictions. Never pretty. Thank God for the collateral custody clause, right? Lets us use kids as leverage. Unpaid rent and so on.' He paused. 'You've not got kids have you?'

I shook my head, terrified. What happened to the children they commandeered?

'That's cool bud, just checking.'

Gasping, I approached the sink for a glass of water. I turned on the tap and it sputtered out brown discharge, grimly reminiscent of Linda's Alcomax skidmarks.

Jasper rose from the bed and approached me. 'That's why I'm here, dude.' he said. He put a hand on my shoulder in a gesture of reassurance, much like the expectant grasp of a predatory uncle. 'I waited in so I could tell you personally. Your water's been put on diversion.'

I almost burst into tears but he squeezed me again.

'I don't want you to worry about this, dude. It's not gonna cost you a penny. Just an implementation fee, some minor plumbing costs, otherwise it's all on us. Okay bro?'

'On diversion?' I said, shaking myself. 'What does that mean? Diverted to where?'

He smiled, pitying and warm. Did he really care about me?

'Down the hall dude. To the bathroom.'

'So I'll need to go to the bathroom every time I need water?'

'That's right,' he said, smiling. 'Another saving.' He nudged me conspiratorially. 'No need to thank me bud.'

'So I'll not need to pay any more water bills?' I said, agog with hope (destructive, unattainable hope).

'That's right,' he said. 'Besides the reservoir subscription and quarterly pipe rental, you can kiss goodbye to water bills for good. How does that feel? Bet you thought you'd be paying those for the rest of your life!'

He stamped the Thrushman's out on the lino, leaving a burn mark that'd inevitably impact my deposit claim. 'Anyway bud, I've gotta be off, just wanted to come by and give you the good news.'

I was so broken I actually whispered *thank you*.

'Sorry bud? Didn't catch that.'

'Thank you.' I said.

He clapped me on the shoulder. 'My pleasure dude, we like to keep our tenants happy. That reminds me.' He reached into his jacket pocket. *Was his suit made from fish skin?* 'Got your latest bill here.'

Without opening it I handed him my debit card, relieved my account was hopelessly overdrawn. (The last bill had equated to six months' wages.)

'You're learning dude!' he said encouragingly. 'So much easier when we all cooperate, right?'

I collapsed on the bed. The property section was still papered to the wall, now faded and mucky (*'one bed units start at £695,000.00'*) and I daydreamed of shower screens and premium wainscoting.

'You thinking of buying a place?' said Jasper, puncturing my reverie. Looking up from the card machine he'd noticed me salivating over housing stability. 'Reckon you'd need, ooh, roughly a seventy grand deposit on one of those,' he said, clocking the picture. 'More if your credit's bad. Plus about thirty grand in stamp duty.'

'A *hundred thousand pounds?*' I said, strangely impressed by the brazenly impenetrable nature of the housing market.

'That's right. That's before you even start paying the mortgage.'

'But,' I said, dumbstruck, 'it'd take me a *lifetime* to save up that much. Where would I find that kind of money?'

'I dunno bud,' he said. 'Got a rich granny?'

I recalled Grandma picking mould nuggets from milk bottles and baking them into green mushroom casseroles. 'No.' I said.

'Better start saving then,' he said. 'Unless you fancy robbing a bank. Or blackmailing a millionaire.'

I laughed, hollow and begloomed.

'Don't sweat it dude. We make our own luck in this world, you know.' he said this with the tireless glee of someone for whom life was unfolding beautifully. 'Looks like your card's been declined bud.' he said. I was immeasurably relieved. Being penniless meant there was nothing for him to take.

'Not a worry dude, I'll come back another time. We'll work something out then.' He zipped up his leather bag and reached down to put his hand on my shoulder. 'Get some rest, okay dude?'

I closed my eyes and prayed for oblivion. I was ruined. Without a job there was no way I could pay next month's rent, nor even begin to clear the rap sheet of charges levied against me. According to the latest bill I was now liable for a 'client liaison transport and presentation fee' which I gathered paid for Jasper's petrol and fishskin suits. The total bill ran into thousands of pounds and the redundancy payout from my last job had dwindled to a cool zero. Besides registering for lousy state benefits there was little I could do to stay afloat.

I *could* borrow from a Gadswood-affiliated loanshark but that'd only hasten my devastation. Their most frequently solicited partner was Sunflower Loans Ltd., an organisation that preyed on the desperate by offering quick loans of up to two thousand pounds. The contract, an impenetrable hundred-page waiver of all consumer rights, stipulated complete autonomy over the user's financial affairs for up to five years, a power they wielded with the recklessness of a cabinet health secretary.

In addition to their own bank details, customers were required to provide those of their parents, partners and friends, all of whom were barraged with terrifying legal threats should a payment be missed or late fee incurred. Incredibly, they were even *more* ruthless than Gadswood's, and were currently under investigation for suspected links to contemporary slavery. As a result of disconnected phone lines, untended inboxes and websites marred by technical faults, contact was achievable only by post, to a forwarding address in Cambodia where all correspondence was re-routed to a municipal waste dump.

Another option was to find a new job, a laughable pipedream now Peter Whamley had succumbed to madness and drink. I hadn't the resources to rob a bank, nor the fortitude to blackmail a millionaire. Should I consult the prosperity gospel?

∞

A knock at the door heaved me from my bed. What new torture was this? Today was my last day at work but the notion of attending was so humiliating I'd snorted nasal mucus when Maltby had mentioned it.

'I'd rather kill myself.' I said, unhesitating.

'Find me in heaven,' he said, flapping his eyelids. 'I'll be on cloud nine.'

I pondered this momentarily. Was he a prophet?

I opened the door to Sheena, her sunken eye sockets now peachy and plumped with face pastes. 'Time for work,' she said, poor fool. 'Why aren't you ready?'

It was then I realised I'd not seen Sheena for two days. Where'd she been?

'I've been sacked,' I said. 'Didn't pass my probation.'

Her mouth convulsed and her eyes dewed with tears. 'What? When?'

'Yesterday,' I said. I closed my eyes and my lip trembled as I whispered, 'I wasn't even allowed to spit on his car.'

Torn, she fussed with her coat sleeves. Evidently she wanted to comfort me but today was her first day and it was vital she met Paul's exacting punctuality standards. 'I'm so sorry,' she said. 'I really have to go. There won't be another bus for an hour. I can't be late on my first day.'

I waved her off, surreptitiously hoping she'd be given the sack too.

'There's a bottle of mouthwash in my room if you need to black out. And some sleeping pills.'

Thanks, I said, thunderously glum.

I shivered as a perishing draft swept through the window. The partition wall, a relatively new erection, was now blackened with mould and wet to the touch. The wood was quickly rotting and I dreaded the charges I'd face to repair it. My bill now covered six pages and included an 'agency recreation subsidy' which, incredibly, covered Jasper's cava intake.

I pulled a blanket around my shoulders and tried to recall when last I was unencumbered by fear of eviction or bankruptcy. A year and a half ago I was, briefly, in a position of power; a management role with a roster of underlings over which I presided like a malevolent god. Thoroughly intoxicated by the power, I'd been granted a glimpse into the worlds of pleasure enjoyed by those in charge. Though brief, it'd set a precedent against which all future endeavours would be measured. I'd shared gin with business directors and crabmeat with department heads, all of which I'd expensed back to the company with little thought for budgetary constraints and beancounting.

Despite the power grabs, bullying and cruelty, I relished my time among the managers. It was a club into which few were permitted but once inside there was little I was denied. I'd seen a board director make two subordinates *fight* for their share of the annual bonus pot (neither was aware he'd already spent it carpeting a house in Toulouse), a horrifying spectacle in spite of the complimentary cheeseboard. Bloodied and tearful, one emerged, victorious, from the beating while the other spent the rest of his life in a wheelchair. When the bonus didn't materialise the winner, devastated by his actions, threw himself from a motorway overpass and was crushed by a Luton van.

'Can't win 'em all.' said the director, walking free after a light slap on the wrists.

Like Solomon Poorfig, I also learnt the dark art of workforce amelioration; that of keeping the grunts subservient with promises of imminent and beneficial cultural improvements. The most effective such strategy was that of the forthcoming 'office refurb'. The office, as it stood at the time, was a spartan concrete outbuilding with temporary cabin toilets and a canteen staffed by embittered young offenders. The floors were dusty with blue linoleum and the fixtures hadn't been replaced in thirty years. The inexhaustible caretaker (may he rest in peace) botched and fiddled his way through an unending charter of repair work, stretched thin on a non-existent budget and hindered by a clutch of tools he'd salvaged from a nearby A road. Meanwhile, staff were given strategic, propitious updates: there'd be a roof terrace, a sun deck, a dining club, a subsidised bar and an executive coffee lounge, all envisioned in glorious CGI renderings. Provided everybody worked like dogs, they said, it'd be done within a year. Naturally the plan bore no fruit whatsoever, being merely a placeholder to increase productivity and ignite trampled morale. Time rolled on and the refurb was quietly edged from the agenda, inconsequential beside staffing announcements and planned charity walkathons. Later it was revealed that, due to budgetary constraints, the whole project had been shelved and there'd be no improvements whatsoever. Comfort could be gleaned, however, from the fact that the refurb committee were negotiating the purchase of a new picnic bench.

During this period I was, by some stretch, the happiest I'd ever been. The entrancing amalgamation of power and financial stability had rendered me amenable and servile, utterly in thrall to my unscrupulous new masters.

The unfortunate truth was that I was gifted the position through a series of happenstantial coincidences; circumstances unimaginable in a democratic recruitment scenario. Unless Paul succumbed to a debilitating addiction and elected me his successor I had no chance of securing that kind of power ever again.

Thoughts of work left me flustered and panting as all the terrors of destitution fizzled and popped before my eyes. I needed to black out.

Sheena's half of the room was accessible through a hole in the wall and was notably smaller than mine. Heartbreakingly, she'd tried making it a little like home by affixing postcards and photographs to the walls, directly contravening Gadswood's 'tacking and wall maintenance' policy (punishable with a replastering fee of up to two thousand pounds) and by filling cups with little pink flowers (*crockery contamination fee: sixty-one pounds*).

There were no windows or cupboards, just a tiny bed

(was it a child's?) with mustard-stained sheets and pillows of sand, besides which stood a tiny unvarnished table. On the table was a heap of property supplements she read as a form of therapeutic torture. Looking closer I noticed that, like a child leafing through catalogues at Christmas, she'd circled particular listings and noted down the plus points of each, as if choosing between underfloor heating and a riverside view was a decision she'd ever have to make.

I found the medicines on a shelf above the bed. The packet advised I take one sleeping pill so I popped three and washed them down with a hearty glug of mouthwash. Replacing the bottle I spied the bag of arsenic, dusty and potent and grey. If only I could've mixed it into one of Paul's yoghurts, I thought.

∞

Sheena's first few weeks at the store were a rapturous frenzy of activity. Paul took her to the Charity & Benefits dinner where she'd been urged to relay her story and emphasise how the company, and Paul in particular, had saved her from destitution and almost certain death. There was an article published about her in the internal magazine (*'Death's Door to Shop Floor'*) and she'd had her photograph taken with the HR director. The story briefly became a matter of local interest when *The Crumbford Examiner* was alerted (Paul again?) and published an article that happily coincided with the opening of the store's new deli counter. She was also paid four hundred pounds by a human tragedy magazine called *Fab!* to disclose details of her gruelling squalor and the debilitating effects of working in a coal pit with a collapsed lung.

The exposure, while thrilling, was fleeting, and petered out within weeks. Jasper had called the day after the story appeared in *Fab!* and demanded Sheena's entire fee, threatening her with eviction if she dared keep one penny of it.

The article also had the galling effect of notifying him of her new job, the spoils of which he took in rent arrears and administrative fees. (She was levied with a 'contractual addendum penalty', a forty-five pound charge to change the 'occupation' field on her tenancy agreement, a cost Jasper laughed off as 'peanuts' to a celebrity like Sheena. 'She probably earns that having a piss.' he said, idly popping a morphine capsule.)

The dwindling media attention brought into focus just how dispiriting the job was. According to Sheena, Paul had become a treacherous, dictatorial monster, more avaricious than I'd ever known him to be.

'He's terrifying,' she said, gnawing on a radish. 'He never leaves his office. Stephen runs his errands for him. Yesterday he made me wash his insoles in the staffroom sink.'

It transpired Paul had also, somewhat incredibly, negotiated a pay *cut* for the contractors, bringing their hourly rate down to below the minimum wage.

'Isn't that illegal?' I said.

'Probably,' she said. 'But there's nothing I can do about it. He'll sack me if I complain.'

I sympathised. Paul had created a climate so oppressive even the most innocuous of grievances felt like a reckless bid for the sack. It seemed the workforce now regularly stabbed each other in the back, reporting to Maltby anything they deemed insubordinate or inflammatory, presumably in an effort to remain in Paul's favour and, ultimately, on the payroll.

'He keeps telling us how much we're being squeezed,' she said. 'Budget cuts and so on. He told us to keep an eye out for anyone not pulling their weight.'

Most remarkably, his dream of a wage-free workforce; that which was seeded with the idea of the teenage interns, had unexpectedly bore fruit. There was now a full-time work experience staffer; a clueless dropout who believed an unpaid six-month stint in a supermarket would bolster their chances of future employment.

'Seriously, he visits soup kitchens, homeless shelters, anywhere people are desperate, and offers them work experience.' She sipped her tea and squeezed her neck (had Paul been demanding piggybacks?). 'He calls it a 'community ingratiation strategy'. There was an article about it in the internal magazine.'

I stared out of the window and noticed a wet trickle snaking down the glass. It was the upstairs neighbour's urine. Foggy from the sleeping pills I genuinely didn't care.

'He's getting a lot of applicants,' she said. 'It's crazy. I don't know how people do it. How do they pay their rent?'

I agreed, previously assuming it was only filmmakers and musicians who worked for nothing.

'How are you?' she said, looking around the room with a sweet, sad smile. Since my dismissal it'd become a gloomy, festering dungeon, grubby with Alcomax miniatures and fecal tissues. I'd been subsisting on rotten vegetables pillaged from the market gutters; scarred carrots and flaying lettuces, and my stomach contracted like a squeezed mophead when I passed excrement. I'd burned through my supply of powdered egg and had been eating weeds I'd torn from cracks in the pavement.

'I'm fine.' I said, a lie even a tabloid reader wouldn't believe.

'Need any more pills?' she said, fishing in her pockets. 'The doctor topped me up.'

'That'd be nice,' I said. I took a small cluster and rattled them like dice. 'Is this enough to kill me?'

'I wouldn't bother,' she said. 'Doctors don't prescribe the good stuff anymore.'

I sighed, utterly exhausted. Sheena wheezed in the cold. I'd run out of tea so we sat in silence and breathed tiresomely.

CHAPTER 25

It was a week later that I was roused from my treacly sorrow. Sheena was banging on the door with slow, agonised thumps, the sound I imagined kidnap victims made before finally succumbing to domination. I daydreamed of being snatched by a firm, malignant kidnapper; of sumptuous meat bones being thrown into a pit where I could live, rent-free, provided I endured intermittent torture and the occasional stab of mutilation.

'What's wrong?' I said, woozy and disinterested.

Her face was pink and she sucked at an inhaler. 'I can't hack it anymore.' she said. Her hands were trembling. Had she just enjoyed a strong coffee? 'Paul's killing me. Can I come in?'

Of course I said, and waved her inside. She seemed to be moving in slow motion. How long had I been asleep?

'Have you got any mouthwash?' she said.

Sorry, no, I said. I'd swallowed the remainder last night (last week?) with some sleeping pills and a pig biscuit. She gulped from a bottle of Alcomax and winced at the burn.

'He's only paying me for two days a week.' she said.

Sounds great, I thought. *More time to drink yourself to death.*

'But he wants me to work the full week.'

I nibbled a lemon rind I'd lifted from the street outside.

'He says that Monday to Friday are my voluntary days, induction time to learn my way around. But the weekends are what I'm paid for.'

'Why not just work the hours you're paid for?' I said.

'Because that makes it look like I'm not a team player. Apparently we all need to pitch in until the new budget's negotiated.'

All lies, I thought. Paul was obviously engaged in a frantic rush to win 'Costsaver of the Year', an annual prize awarded to the store that showed the most shameless contempt for its workers and their rights. The winner received not only a laminated certificate but also a voucher to spend instore. For Paul, however, the real prize far exceeded paltry grocery coupons. Being recognised in such a way meant another step towards promotion, validation, respect. Perhaps an extra day's holiday somewhere down the line.

'He's going to destroy me,' she said. 'I'm worse off than my muckraking days.'

She stared at the sleet machine-gunning the window. Outside was dark and tombstone grey.

'We could give him the arsenic,' I said, trying to cheer her up. 'Slip it into his milk.'

She laughed, briefly elated. 'It'd be great to see him really ill.' Her smile receded. 'But it wouldn't solve anything. A few weeks off, a comfy hospital bed, free food, sounds like we'd be doing him a favour.'

Resignedly I agreed. It'd be heartening to see him vomiting blood but inevitably he'd seek treatment and return stronger, the spell in hospital used to plan a slew of new initiatives.

'Plus it wouldn't help the financial situation,' she said. 'He's hardly going to approve pay rises if he thinks he's been poisoned.' She paused. 'Not that he'd do it anyway, of course.'

'What about blackmail?' I said, recalling Jasper's suggestion. 'That might tide us over for a while.'

'What do you mean?' she said. 'Blackmail Paul? I'm not sure he's that well off. Have you seen his *clothes?*'

I recalled the tired fleeces and boxy hiking jackets. 'Might be nice to inconvenience him though wouldn't it, even for a little while?'

Her eyes narrowed and her fists tensed. She stared at the advert papered to the wall and sucked the inhaler. 'What if we blackmailed the *store?*'

She said this quietly. She was serious. 'Remember when people used to do that? In the nineties, put glass in baby food? Happened all the time.'

'Yes, vaguely.' I said.

She was standing now, pacing the room with the insistence of one struck by true inspiration.

'How would we do it?' I said, galvanised by any scheme that'd drag the company's name through the mud.

'We wouldn't actually *do* it,' she said. 'I don't want to kill any babies, do you?'

No, I said. Had she asked whether I'd feel comfortable poisoning ordinary Saturday shoppers my answer would've been an unapologetic *yes.*

'We'd just have to *tell* them we'd done it. Do you know what I mean?'

'So why do we need the arsenic?' I said. I felt my stomach lurch.

She rolled her eyes. 'To prove we can do it.'

Oh, I said, not quite comprehending.

She continued: 'we'd send them a demand; tell them we've poisoned something in the store. They're far more likely to take us seriously if we send them some actual poison, right? Something like *'there's more where this came from'*, that kind of thing.'

I stared at her. There was no denying it, she'd made up her mind. 'Okay,' I said. 'How much would we ask for?'

She tilted her head to the newspaper on the wall. '£695,000.00 sounds alright,' she said. 'Enough to buy one of those flats. Get out of this place, start again. What do you think? No more Jasper, no more fees...' she tailed off as if into a dream. 'Can you imagine?'

Foolishly I permitted myself a momentary glimpse of hope. Housing stability would grant me the freedom to choose an actual *career* and not veer blindly from one demeaning, temporary appointment to the next. I could accumulate savings, pay into a pension, perhaps even treat myself to some premium cashmere.

'You're thinking about it,' said Sheena, noting my thin, guarded smile. 'I can tell. You want to do this.'

She was right. Short of a lottery win or fabricated compensation payout, it seemed the only feasible means of escape. Morally I had no reservations whatsoever (defrauding a supermarket was as irreproachable as firebombing an MP's second home), my concern was the degree to which Paul might suffer. 'Would it actually *hurt* him?' I said, his misery my absolute number one priority.

'That store's everything to him,' she said. 'Imagine if it fell into disrepute. Imagine if it *closed*.' She unpeeled this last word with a delicious, irresistible zeal. It was like she'd risen anew; her hatred for Paul a screaming, catalytic flashbomb.

'Where would we send it?' I said. 'To his office?'

She shook her head. 'He'd throw it in the bin, ignore it. We need to make it public. Get the newspapers involved. They need to know it's happening because of him. Because of his greed. Because of the way he treats people.'

She was trembling now, giddy with the strength attainable only through extreme personal peril. Despite its infancy Sheena seemed to have mapped out every detail of the scheme.

'What'll the message say?' I said.

She paused, drumming her fingers against the fishtank. 'Something like, *as penance for the greed and*, er, *callousness shown towards his employees, Paul,* what's his other name?'

'Meakins.' I said.

'*Paul Meakins must now face the consequences of his actions.*' She flexed her jawbone like a prize fighter. She was happier than I'd ever seen her.

'Then something like, *hundreds of products have now been contaminated with the enclosed poison. You have no way of knowing what they are.*' She stopped, idled momentarily, then with maniacal relish: '*Hundreds of innocent people will convulse, vomit and die. This is preventable if the company does the right thing.'* She stopped to catch her breath and fanned her florid cheeks. 'Then we'll ask for the money, tell them where to deliver it, blah blah blah. What do you think?'

She'd presented an exquisite case. The fact Paul was called out by name thrilled me enormously and I hoped he might kill himself over the matter. I envisaged his body, lifeless and stiff, swinging from a crossbeam, eyes bulging from their throttled sockets and a suicide note thanking the supermarket for the opportunities they'd provided him.

'Sounds good to me,' I said. 'How'll they deliver the money? Do we just ask for a binbag full of cash?'

She fell silent. 'That'll be tricky,' she said. 'We could be spotted collecting it. Let me think about that one.'

We spent the evening entrenched in the minutiae of criminal activity: teaspoons and tweezers meticulously filtering the arsenic into a fresh bag, ensuring it was fibre and fingerprint-free (would they bother checking such things?) and drafting the blackmail letter. Sheena had removed mention of the employees, reasoning that'd unfavourably narrow down the list of perpetrators, instead focusing on his treatment of customers, superiors, anyone he might've had contact with.

The issue of payment was addressed by a colleague of Sheena's. A fretful little boglin from the coal pit who used the dark web to procure recreational drugs, he'd agreed to let us use his anonymous cryptocurrency account to receive and facilitate the ransom, a service he offered in exchange for a back rub and ten thousand pounds, trousered on receipt of the balance.

'It'll be worth it,' said Sheena. 'It's totally untraceable.'

Fine, I said, clueless about the intricacies of computing (what did HTML even *mean?*) and quietly begrudging of its centralised role in the world. My only gripe was the fee, which seemed inordinately high for such a low-risk administrative procedure. Sheena, as ever, talked me round: 'it sounds like a fortune,' she said. 'But it wouldn't even cover the deposit on a house boat.'

We used Peter Whamley's computer to print the letter, handling it with gloves to avoid stray fingerprints and incriminating skin cells. The arsenic was carefully enclosed and the packages sealed into a satisfying little bundle. We were, in fact, sending three letters: one to *The Crumbford Examiner*, one to the company's head office and one to Paul himself. We reasoned the newspaper, a hateful mouthpiece for anti-immigration propaganda that'd been reprimanded by a media regulator after demanding the drowned corpses of asylum seekers be used as cattlefeed (*'Freedom of Moo-vement'*), would leap on the story, seizing on the notion of unknowable forces threatening the British service industry.

In the unlikely event they ignored it, the letter to head office would surely speed the process along, reaching the legal team directly and ensuring we were dealt with quickly and with minimal outcry.

We arranged for the letters to arrive on a Monday in an effort to ensure maximum panic. Sheena had assured me this was when Paul was at his most pervasive and needling, a strategy he used to weed out those compromised by the joys of the weekend. (The poor souls singled out were sacked as soon as Paul could conjure a plausible enough reason. One contractor was dismissed for 'lavatorial misconduct', an officious term for leaving a troublesome skidmark.)

Having completed the act of blackmail we toasted our good work with a half litre of Alcomax.

'Do you think they'll pay up?' I said.

Sheena's eyes reddened after a bracing swig. 'I do actually,' she said with a cautious smile. 'I think we're going to get away with it.'

Despite being based solely on blind hope, her confidence was heartening. It was then I realised that at no point during the process had I ever envisioned being caught, possibly because I believed what we were doing was fundamentally right, undeserving of punitive measures of any kind. Were I the investigating officer it'd take five seconds with Paul to know his persecutors deserved at the very least a pat on the back, if not full and immediate remuneration.

We stayed up all night, talking through the life-altering opportunities afforded by home ownership.

'Did people always have to do this?' said Sheena. 'I mean, how did people afford homes in the past?'

Drunk and ill-informed, I explained how the property market hadn't always been a money pit used by landlords to fleece the poor and the desperate. Supposedly banks had once granted mortgages to those who needed a place to live, not merely an asset in which to bury their accumulated wealth.

'Sounds far-fetched to me.' she said, snorting incredulously.

I tried to explain that there was a time, not so long ago, when teachers, postmen, even *nurses*, could afford their own homes.

'Ha! Sounds like you've had too much of this stuff.' She waved the Alcomax bottle at me. 'How's a *nurse* going to afford a house? Selling pills on the black market?'

I agreed, it sounded *incredible*, but astonishingly there was a time when criminality wasn't the only means by which to house oneself.

She took a swig and scoffed, disbelieving of my proto-communist rhetoric. 'You'd still have to save up a deposit though, right? How would you do that if all your wages went on rent?'

Feeling like I was quoting from a thousand year old scroll, I explained that, in the past, rent made up a far smaller fraction of one's outgoings.

Again she laughed, utterly uncomprehending.

I continued, now unsure I even believed the words coming out of my mouth. 'The government also gave poorer people council houses,' I said. 'So they paid even less rent.'

At this she almost choked, clutching her throat as her eyes streamed with tears. I felt like I was reeling off a list of weird jokes. 'Surely that's an urban myth,' she said. 'Why would the government bother helping anyone? What's in it for them?'

I agreed, it was laughable that a ruling party would care a jot for its underlings, as keeping them poor and docile seemed, ironically, the best way to win votes.

She took a punishing gulp and lowered her eyes, dismissive of my fairytales. 'Whatever,' she said. 'None of that matters now. We're going to be *free*, do you understand? Free from rent, mortgages, all that shit. Can you even imagine?'

It was a conversation we'd had many times, a gleeful exchange of fantasies wherein we listed everything we'd do if unshackled from renting costs. Sheena dreamt of holidays, the most fleeting and wasteful of luxuries, while I wisely coveted chrome-plated kitchen gadgets that'd put an end to hand mashing and butter whisks.

The bottle finished, Sheena gobbled a sleeping pill and crashed out on the floor, untroubled by the oncoming hangover or Paul's inevitable reprimand.

'He can rot in hell.' she said, vindicating my every wish.

∞

If we'd worried about being ignored, we'd been fools. The front page of Tuesday's *Crumbford Examiner* shrieked uproariously about the *'terror death plague'* that'd befallen the store, smearing Paul's name so viciously I almost wept with joy. In the letter we'd divulged titbits about the cruelty and malpractice over which he'd presided; mostly non-incriminating generalities that could be fact-checked by even the laziest tabloid journalist. Evidently the *Examiner* hadn't bothered doing even this, preferring riotous hyperbole that labelled Paul a 'fascist fatcat' and the company a 'hateful hotbed of corruption'. Board directors were profiled, their credentials scrutinised in an effort to glean evidence of incompetence and links to terrorist organisations. The HR director, in particular, was savaged so brutally (*'A Calamitous*

Catalogue of Failure'), I predicted a suicide obituary would soon appear in the very same paper.

The ultimate decimation, however, was reserved for Paul. It seemed we'd served them a pitch-perfect narrative of corruption, fear and revenge, a clutch of threads they quickly wove into a world-exclusive exposé of sickening corporate greed.

That evening Sheena skittered in, flapping at me with the paper. 'Have you seen this?' she said, her sparrow arms whirling like stalks. 'They love it!'

Not wanting to miss out on such a story, rival publications had leapt on it and within days it'd become a national concern.

A local television network ran a feature, an unexpectedly sympathetic piece about the consequences of corporate irresponsibility, and managed to source a number of employees sacked at Paul's behest, the most vocal of which was Linda. She'd granted the news crew access to her living room, deliberately left filthy to illicit maximum viewer sympathy, and was interviewed beside Aunt Tasmin, her mouth peeled like a flatfish and her arms sagging like deflated balloons.

'I knew something was up,' she said, her teeth jagged and unevenly spaced. 'When he brought in all them zero hours contractors.' This sounded stunted and rehearsed but was enough of a development that the next day the *Examiner* ran a front-page splash about inhumane working conditions and blue collar slavery. (Zero hours contracts had become dicey territory for businesses, their impermanent nature a contributing factor in social inequality and upward immobility. Still bafflingly legal, any company reliant on wholesome family branding had distanced themselves from the practice, deeming the PR risks too great when weighed against the superficial cost savings.)

Paul's implementation of such methods was picked through in forensic detail. The *Examiner* drafted in employment consultants to ratify the outrage expressed in their thinkpieces, all of them furious that a company would exploit their workers so cruelly. By dizzying coincidence, Solomon Poorfig was probed, his association with Whamley & Poorfig and knowledge of the sector proving fertile ground for a corroborative soundbite.

'It's completely reprehensible,' he said, hilariously unfazed by the interns' blood on his hands. 'People need job security and employers they can trust.'

Amidst all the frenzy and furore, the strangest convolution was the lack of condemnation for our supposed act of terror. The media had almost unanimously decided it was the company and their exploitative labour practices that were to blame, portraying us as vigilante heroes crusading for the justice our overlords had so brazenly disregarded.

The prevailing narrative held that the company would simply close the store and pay the ransom, writing it off as the cost of bad business. The headlines even stated as much (*Supermarket Sweep - Store Stung for 600k*), assuming our reward was an unquestionable certainty. Sheena remained cautious, however. She'd not uncork the mouthwash, she said, until the money had been safely received. Her colleague at the coal pit had yet to confirm payment and I was concerned he'd simply pocket the cash and flee to the seaside.

Three days passed and the coverage continued to blossom. The *Examiner* had sourced pictures of Salman's recent turd sabotage and called for an immediate boycott of the store, demanding to know why it hadn't been closed months ago.

'It's incredible,' said Sheena, buoyant after a lackadaisical shift. 'The place is empty. No customers. Nothing to do.'

Naturally this filled me with joy, the thought of Paul's miserable face and blackened name providing some consolation for my previous indignity. 'How is he?' I said, dearly hoping he'd cut his wrists in a bath of cold milk.

She looked at me with a smile like a lemon segment. 'Terrible.' she said. Her eyes watered in a sudden rush of emotion. She beamed. 'He's broken.'

CHAPTER 26

What happened next was confounding. Having been led to believe we'd receive our ransom without so much as a cursory quibble, the next day's *Examiner* led with the headline '*Arsonicked - Supermarket Poisoners Foiled.*' The article claimed the tampered items had been located and destroyed, apparently with the help of sniffer dogs. Beneath was a photograph of Paul, grinning and smart, proclaiming the threat had been neutralised and the public had nothing to fear. As a gesture of goodwill and a reward for ongoing brand loyalty, he was offering five percent off deli meats for the first fifty shoppers to return to the store.

'That's how much I value my customers.' he said.

I threw the paper at the wall, furious with disappointment. The single glimmer of hope (cruel, unsinkable hope) that'd kept my spirits aglow was now extinguished, trampled to mulch like Grandma's graveside dandelions. Such failure shouldn't have come as a surprise, however, the most recent years of my life had comprised little beyond crushing disappointment and unparalleled sadness. Why might this, of all things, have ended differently?

I gobbled the remaining sleeping tablets and retched down a gargle of mouthwash. *I hope I never wake up,* I thought, as the room began to billow and flounder.

I didn't dream, of course, instead shifting about the bed like an underfed grub. Nor, sadly, did I die, waking to a hysterical banging at the door. I pulled my eyes open and rose. Thank heavens my bank account was empty, I thought, fearing Jasper and his portable card machine. Was my rent overdue? I was so mired in debt I had no idea what had and hadn't been paid.

I opened the door and Sheena leapt at me, flinging her arms around my neck. She thrust her head into my chest and wept. I led her inside where she continued crying furiously. Could I purify her tears into drinking water? She'd evidently seen the story in the *Examiner* and was as crushed as I'd been. What was left for us now? Chasing rats in prison?

'I can't believe it.' she said, finally taking a breath. Her shoulders were trembling.

'I know,' I said. 'Apparently they used sniffer dogs.'

She looked at me with eyes like radishes. 'What are you talking about?'

I fetched the newspaper and folded open the front page. She read it in silence, her small mouth busily shaping and moulding the words.

'At least we tried,' I said, hoping I sounded comforting. 'At least we caused Paul some upset.'

Very quickly she reached into her coat pocket and pulled out a sheet of paper. She handed it to me with trembling fingers and a smile like a portcullis.

'What's this?' I said. 'More fees?'

Clearly relishing the suspense (couldn't you just *tell* me, Sheena?) she shook her head. 'Open it.'

I unfolded the letter and noted the bank's logo in the top right-hand corner. Reflexively I went to screw it up but Sheena held my arm, urging me to read on. It was a bank statement, the likes of which I received every month and had wisely stopped opening. (Unfathomably they penalised me for exceeding my overdraft limit, a spiteful surcharge that inched me further into insolvency).

I scanned the page, stopping dead at the available balance. I looked back at her.

'Is this,' I didn't know what to say.

She nodded, flushed and smiling. 'Minus the handling fee.'

The figure was £685,000.00.

Shocked from my fug, I quickly regained my senses and rose to attention.

'I don't understand,' I said, still staring at the statement. 'What about this?' I showed her the newspaper.

She beamed and let out a clipped little laugh. 'That's just PR,' she said. 'Damage control. They want to be seen to be doing something about it. Keeps the public on side.'

I was concerned such proactivity would reflect positively on Paul, maybe even net him a bonus for reaching a swift resolution.

'But he didn't,' she reminded me. 'If that was the case they wouldn't have paid us off. They can't be seen to be giving in to blackmail.'

The ransom note had stated that once the money was safely deposited all the tampered items would be removed, anonymously, and destroyed. They'd have no way of knowing when this would occur but we'd guaranteed no customers would be harmed. We'd been deliberately vague on this last point, hoping they'd take our word for it and assume we had some elaborate surveillance system in place. It was a risk that, miraculously, seemed to have worked.

CHAPTER 27

Sheena had arranged a viewing at the Drillfield Quays development and had already begun throwing her possessions (grey cups, an old soap dish) into binbags. Neither of us owned much given the dearth of storage space so most of our packing was done in the time it took to boil an egg.

We'd resolved, very wisely, to vacate the property without paying a penny of our back rent, much less the fees for which we were liable.

'They're lucky we don't burn the place to the ground.' said Sheena, looking very much like she'd do so in a heartbeat.

∞

The Drillfield Quays development was glorious. Set among shipping containers and sprawling suicide piers, it rose from the landscape like a stately hernia. As with all modern erections, it'd been constructed predominantly from glass and allowed floor-to-ceiling views of the residents' bedrooms, a design initiative presumably intended to titillate randy longshoremen.

Sheena skipped and twirled, resplendent in a new lambswool pullover, and sipped a tin of pop.

'Look at that,' she said, extending her arm in an explanatory motion. 'How do you fancy living *there?*'

It was a bright, balmy day and the place looked wonderful. I envisaged myself padding between rooms, cradling a steaming espresso (I'd need to procure a new machine since the old one had rusted useless) and surveying the passing ships, perhaps stepping out to the balcony to pinch one of Sheena's Thrushman's.

'When's the agent arriving?' I said, delirious at the prospect of a cash buy. How I'd laud my wealth over everyone I'd meet!

'Any time now,' she said. 'Don't worry, they're scum. They're always late.'

I scarfed the remainder of my prawn crumpet, relishing the taste of luxury as it funnelled down my throat. It'd cost £7.95 – more than last month's entire food budget.

On closer inspection, the building seemed almost comically incongruous. There were no bars or businesses nearby, in fact there was very little in the vicinity to justify the exorbitant price tag. Sheena noticed my sneering and explained: 'there used to be a tower block here,' she said. 'I think about two hundred people lived in it.'

I looked up at the metallic balconies and the glassed, silent rooms.

'Don't worry, they're gone now,' she said, sipping her drink. 'Most of them died in a fire a few years ago.'

I'd read about the Drillfield dockyard fire. In order to meet the spiralling gentrification demands of the surrounding area, the local council had imposed on their tenants hilariously unreasonable rent increases, threatening with eviction anyone who couldn't pay up. This met with such fierce opposition they were forced to retreat, issuing a humiliating retraction that guaranteed the security of those they'd deigned to house.

Much like Paul's strategy for ousting Linda, however, the scorned councilmen had a contingency plan. Through a systematic programme of underfunding and neglect, life in the block became so nightmarish many tenants were driven to throw themselves off the roof.

Fire precautions were sidelined and safety checks forgotten as the residents were flushed out like troublesome rats. ('Expendable scum' was the term one councillor used.)

A year later, after innumerable protests and leafleting campaigns, an electrical fire engulfed the block and silenced all remaining dissent. The land was quickly sold to a developer and the charred residents rehoused in a converted cow shed seventy miles away. 'Gets them out of our hair.' reasoned the councillor.

A blobby little hatchback rolled around the corner and for a brief, terrifying moment I froze, thinking it was Jasper behind the wheel.

'Don't worry, it's not him.' said Sheena, taking my arm.

The agent who met us, a bristling playboy named Stu, was tanned, chiselled and immaculate. He greeted us with a smile like a catalogue model. 'Hey guys,' he said, his voice warm like caramel. 'So sorry to keep you waiting.'

Like smokers' penises we wilted under his gaze, utterly intoxicated by such charisma. I had to remind myself that, despite his magnetism, he was an estate agent, and thus worthy of only our basest contempt.

He shook our hands warmly. 'Shall we go inside?'

Thank you, I said, though I didn't know why.

Predictably, the flat was beautiful. Thick wooden doors led between rooms decorated in leather and pastel and the floors were varnished a rich honey brown. The ceilings were studded with recessed downlights that twinkled when undimmed, saturating the walls with pristine white light.

Stu uncorked a bottle of champagne and poured us each a glass (would this incur a fee?), advising we make ourselves at home.

'Kick off your shoes guys, have a roll in the beds if you like.' He waved a dismissive hand. 'Only joking! Seriously though, make yourselves at home. Anything you want, just ask.'

In the living room was a refreshments table on which was laid out a dizzying spread of canapés and pressed juice. I folded a nubbin of beef into my mouth and hesitated before taking another.

'Go ahead,' said Stu, noting my restraint. 'Have as many as you like. Everything's free.'

We fluttered from room to room, glugging champagne and listening as Stu enthused about the building. It was, more or less, meaningless waffle, yet the difference in tone was unmistakable. Unlike with Jasper, we were now being offered discounts, having fees waived, even being promised complimentary gifts ('I'll throw in a case of Beaujolais,' said Stu. 'Just because I like you guys.')

I'd been concerned that, despite our well-deserved windfall, we didn't actually have enough cash to meet the asking price. Various outgoings had been incurred since we were paid. Sheena's weakness for lambswool had made a not-insignificant dent in our capital ('it feels like Grandpa's moustache'), while I'd spent a small fortune on algae pads for the fishtank. I needn't have worried, however, as Stu was prepared to go a full fifty thousand pounds below the asking price.

'One of the perks of paying cash.' he said.

The sale was finalised within a week. Given the flat was vacant and we were chain-free first time buyers, it was as straightforward as such transactions were possible to get. I'd panicked briefly about credit ratings until Sheena reminded me we weren't applying for a mortgage and thus it made no difference.

'It'll be like buying a packet of biscuits.' she said, and unexpectedly it was.

∞

Standing in Stu's office with two binliners at our feet we were poured more champagne and clapped on the shoulders by kindly colleagues. Stu appeared and presented us a cellophaned hamper bursting with soap and fruit cheeses.

'Just a little something to say well done,' he said, shaking our hands. 'You guys deserve it.'

We signed some meaningless forms and adjourned to the

212

car.

'I wanted to drive you myself,' he said with a smile. 'You guys feel like friends.'

On the drive to the quays we passed Gadswood's office and I felt a gnaw of unease as I recalled the money we owed them, none of which we had any intention of paying back. We'd left no forwarding address (I was understandably terrified of post) and done our best to destroy the bedsit in an honourable and justifiable act of subterfuge. I'd smashed the cracked windowpane, reducing it to smithereens while Sheena had demolished the adjoining wall, ripping through it with a claw hammer and tears in her eyes. We tore up linoleum, knocked holes in walls, yanked out gas pipes and wiped excrement across the ceiling in a furious, cathartic upswell of violence. Had Jasper been present I doubt he'd have escaped without a hammer blow to the skull.

Thankfully my parents were dead and Sheena's mum was in prison, meaning Gadswood's had little chance of recouping the cost of the damages. They could, in theory, chase Sheena's employers for the debt, forcibly siphoning it off her wages each month like a bloodthirsty local council, but ultimately it'd prove fruitless. 'Who cares?' she said. 'I don't mind taking a pay cut. It's not like I *need* the job, right?'

She *was* right. Now that we owned property, anything we earned, however miniscule, was ours to keep. I'd even considered a job as a public servant to earn some extra pocket money.

We arrived at the quays and rode the lift to our new apartment. Inside was gleaming (Stu had had it cleaned, of course) and greeting us on the countertop was a huge bouquet of flowers, majestic in peach and lilac. Beside it sat the coveted case of Beaujolais, its bottles black and gleaming in the light.

'Just our little gift to you.' said Stu, handing over two sets of keys. They each glittered with a brushed metal keyring, a miniature rendering of the building itself.

'Those were specially commissioned by the developer,'

said Stu, swinging the little ornaments. 'Real sterling silver. Just a little thank you.'

I'd been thanked, congratulated and rewarded so often over the last few weeks, usually with little to no justification, that I'd begun to believe that maybe I *did* deserve to be showered in adulation and gifts. I had, after all, taken the noble step of blackmailing my salacious employer, successfully co-masterminding a scheme that'd enabled me to enjoy a bountiful, rent-free existence, unstrung from the shackles of minionhood and accountable to no one. Perhaps I should give lectures on the art of success?

'Honestly guys, it's been such a pleasure working with you,' said Stu, humbly accepting the glass of wine Sheena thrust at him. 'If there's anything I can do to help, just ask. I'm always on the end of a phone.'

We toasted the finalised purchase and saw Stu to the door. In place of the usual handshake he gave us both a thick paternal hug. As he drew me close I smelt his musky aftershave and again said *thank you,* though this time I meant it.

CHAPTER 28

Sheena stayed on at the supermarket, primarily not to arouse suspicion but also to cover any bills that appeared. (Hilariously we'd gone months without paying a single bill because I'd gotten so used to throwing them in the bin. It was only after the gas wouldn't light that it occurred to us there might be a problem.)

Now her home life was secure, Sheena claimed to actually *enjoy* work, a mindset seemingly at odds with all logical thought.

'I feel free,' she said. 'I can make mistakes, I can take sick days, I can stand up for myself, and I won't lose my home. There's nothing they can do to me.'

Paul, conversely, was a wreck. The board of directors was in the process of expediting his dismissal and he'd been hauled to employment tribunals by several former employees, the most savage of which was Linda's. While the public outcry had abated, the internal investigation was tightening to an almost tortuous degree – he'd been charged with managerial misconduct, negligence, even human rights violations. Sheena recounted his decline with wild-eyed elation: the snake of solicitors outside his office, the hours worked too late, the rust spotting his wheel arches (unconnected but welcome), all as he tried to salvage some crumbs of respect, morsels of goodwill that'd somehow allow him to keep his job.

Hearteningly, it was a hopeless fantasy. Head office employed a swift and brutal dismissal policy with disgraced colleagues, doubly so if the media had gotten involved. (One store manager was caught by an undercover film crew calling the CEO a 'dopey old twat' and was sacked on the spot. Disavowed by the company and denied redundancy pay under threat of prosecution, he was unable to find legitimate work elsewhere. Penniless and desperate, he'd fallen in with an Uzbekistani slave trader and taken a job trafficking migrants through treacherous European territories. Speaking at his funeral, his mother condemned him as 'an abomination...a waste of bloody space.')

I willed Paul a similar fate. If Sheena's dispatches were any indication, it appeared he was nearing his end, disgraced, discredited and with scant hope of redemption.

∞

It was spring. The light was softening and there'd been a fluctuation in interest rates, whatever the hell that meant. This led Sheena to investigate the possibility of securing a bank loan; capital we'd use to buy a second property to rent out at a sizeable profit.

'Imagine what we'd do with the extra cash,' she said, grinning vampishly. 'You could buy that magnetic knife block we talked about.'

We were draped over the balcony like keeled slugs, half drunk on gin and chainsmoking Thrushman's. I was languorous and amenable, staring out over the quays with my arms hanging loose over the railing.

'Why not?' I said. 'Sounds good to me.'

She was leafing through bank pamphlets, all of which featured smiling liars inviting customers to pay more per month to access their own money.

'We could get an equity release on this place,' she said, rapping her knuckles against the glass. 'Seems pretty straightforward.'

It was then that the stillness of the evening was broken. A distant engine sound revved from the dock road, swelling as it drew nearer. I squinted as the car came into view, toy-sized from our vantage point.

'Is that a sailor?' I said. *Did sailors drive cars?*

Sheena joined me at the railing, spilling a little of her drink. (Admirably, she'd been drinking since lunchtime). 'Seems weird,' she said. 'There aren't any boats.'

The car turned off the road and onto the cargo pier. It looked familiar but was too far away to place.

'Is that who I think it is?' said Sheena.

I knew exactly who she meant. The car, now a tiny spot among the stacked shipping containers, had stopped at the end of the pier. We watched. A figure emerged from the vehicle, shuffling and indistinct. I gulped my gin, the stiff wet taste bracing and cold. The figure shut the car door and headed towards the pier edge.

'Is he fishing?' I said, fully aware he wasn't.

The figure stood, small as an insect, at the edge of the structure. It was twenty metres down and the water was perishing.

'He's going to jump.' said Sheena, slurping off the remainder of her drink.

She was right. After several seconds of statuesque contemplation, the figure threw itself headfirst off the edge. We watched as the body, lumpen and flaccid, hit the water with an inconsequential splash. Within a second it'd disappeared.

'Told you.' she slurred.

To our surprise a second figure then emerged from the car, taller and stockier than the first. He strode to the edge and peered off the side, waiting a full two minutes before returning to the car, closing the door and driving back towards the road. I stared hard as the car passed the front of the building, dented and spotted with rust, and for the briefest of moments glimpsed Stephen Maltby behind the wheel.

∞

Not long after Paul's suicide I received a call from Peter Whamley's office. Had he finally succumbed to his demons?

'Long time no see, y'bastard!' he said, sounding surprisingly well. 'Guess who's back in business, eh?'

It transpired head office had reinstated Whamley as their primary recruitment consultant, requesting he restaff the Prawnmoor store after 'the Paul debacle'.

'Can't speak ill of the dead but that were a nasty little bastard,' he said, his voice moist with tea. 'Never did trust him.'

Idly I sucked a Thrushman's and ran a finger over the brushed steel of the knife block. What do you *want,* Whamley?

'Anyway, anyway, I've got a proposition for ya,' he said. 'How d'you fancy your old job back?'

I stared at the bank statement stuck to the fridge. Our tenants' rent more than covered our monthly outgoings, leaving heaps in the bank for Grenache and sardine hampers.

I paused, relishing the heartbeats. 'No thanks,' I said. 'I'm fine for work.'

We exchanged some final pleasantries (he'd been undergoing maggot therapy) before I hung up and returned to the balcony. Sheena handed me a drink; a pink gin with a raspberry bobbing in it.

'Who was that?' she said.

'No one.' I said, quietly drifting off to sleep.

THE END

Printed in Great Britain
by Amazon